"Maybe that █████████ **so easy for** ███████

"You mean, it was easy for *you* to get," Candice said.

"Me? What are you talking about? I didn't get any annulment. In fact, I never even got a copy of the papers from you," J.T. said.

Candice closed her eyes tightly, light-headedness coming with a vengeance. "What?" she whispered.

"You got the annulment," he stated.

She reached for the elevator doorjamb and tried to think. "No, you said..." She tried to remember what both of them had said on that fateful night eight years ago.

"No, I agreed to it and said, if you wanted it, to get it," he clarified, his eyes narrowing. Then an odd smile touched his lips.

Candice wasn't smiling. "J.T.?" she said softly, but couldn't focus on him. He blurred and shimmered before her as the light-headedness took over for good this time.

She grasped at the elevator door frame to ground herself, but it didn't do any good. She was floating, and her last thought before she fainted dead away was that life had just played its cruelest card.

She was still married to J.T....

Dear Reader,

"You don't own a tux shop for forty years and not know something about romance." So says Karl Delaney...and he's about to prove it for three bachelor buddies who have the fortune to rent from his shop. These three friends are about to get some BIG surprises!

Mary Anne Wilson concludes the DELANEY'S GROOMS trilogy with *Cowboy in a Tux*. The full-time novelist lives with her husband in Southern California, near her children and grandchildren.

If you missed any of the DELANEY'S GROOMS books, you can order #769 *Suddenly a Daddy* by Mindy Neff and #774 *The Last Two Bachelors* by Linda Randall Wisdom. Send $3.99 ($4.50 in Canada), plus 75¢ postage and handling ($1.00 in Canada) for each book ordered, to: Harlequin Reader Service, 3010 Walden Ave., P.O. Box 1325, Buffalo NY 14269 or, in Canada, to: P.O. Box 609, Fort Erie, Ont. L2A 5X3.

Happy reading!

Debra Matteucci
Senior Editor & Editorial Coordinator
Harlequin Books
300 East 42nd Street
New York, NY 10017

Cowboy in a Tux

MARY ANNE WILSON

TORONTO • NEW YORK • LONDON
AMSTERDAM • PARIS • SYDNEY • HAMBURG
STOCKHOLM • ATHENS • TOKYO • MILAN • MADRID
PRAGUE • WARSAW • BUDAPEST • AUCKLAND

ISBN 0-373-16778-4

COWBOY IN A TUX

Look us up on-line at: http://www.romance.net

Printed in U.S.A.

Prologue

"I think the caption said, 'The Cowboy and His Filly,' but I could be wrong."

J. T. Watson held his cell phone to his ear as he entered the elevator just off the conference room of the Hombley Towers, where merger talks had gone on for a marathon twelve hours. He was sick and tired of them. Sick and tired of having people bluff him, lie to him and try to manipulate him. So he'd said he'd be in touch, stood and walked out.

He'd barely made it into the reception area before the cell phone had rung, and Jack O'Connor had been on the other end of the line. It was a welcome surprise to hear from one of the few people in this life that he counted as a good friend. At least it was until Jack had mentioned the article in the newspaper.

"You called me in London to tell me what some rag said about me?" he commented as he strode across to the bank of elevators.

"Hey, it's news here. Sandi showed it to me. You and that model, the single-name beauty, Vanny or

Vonny or Veggie, you made the front page of the Life section in San Francisco. Pretty damn serious stuff, if you ask me. And a notch above that ice skater you were dancing with last year.''

''The ice skater was one date where there happened to be a reporter nearby. And the one-name model's name is Vonya.'' He repeated it slowly by syllables as he stepped into the middle elevator. ''Von…ya, and I'm sure she'll be thrilled to be called a horse.''

Jack laughed at that. ''I bet she's a knockout even when she's angry. All that wild black hair, and what is she, six feet tall?''

''Close enough. She's about two inches shorter than I am,'' J.T. said as the doors slid shut.

''And it's not a one-date thing, is it?''

''We see each other when we can,'' he said, looking at his image bouncing back at him off the highly polished surface of the doors. ''She says she gets a kick out of being seen with a cowboy.'' He narrowed his hazel eyes on his reflection.

A white, band-collared shirt worn with a casual suede jacket, fringed on the arms and the yoke, scrubbed blue jeans and custom-made boots. A white Stetson partially shaded his face, a face that was all angles and planes, tanned from being outside on the ranch, yet etched with lines from the long, hard bargaining session.

''And you don't mind being seen with a towering beauty.''

''Who would?''

''You're right.''

''Is this all you've got to do, call me in London

to ask me about who I'm dating? I don't give you hell about your love life.''

"You won't be able to, either, because I'm getting married.''

J.T. pushed the button for the parking garage, and the elevator started its thirty-floors descent. ''This must be a bad connection. I thought you said you were getting married.''

"You heard right. Married, as in forever, head-over-heels-in-love type of marriage. First Dylan, now me. Who knows, you might be next with that one-name model.''

Jack, Dylan Montgomery and J.T. had been friends since college, as close as brothers. And every bit as different.

"Don't hold your breath," J.T. said on a chuckle. "I've never been in the same league as the two of you.''

That was a basic truth among the three of them. Dylan was old money, Jack was new money with class, and J.T., well... He didn't have to glance down at his Levi's and boots to know who and what he was. A sixth-generation Texan, brought up dirt poor for sixteen years, until his father figured out how to make a better mousetrap. But in their case, the better mousetrap had been a way to manufacture delicate circuitries at half the cost, twice the profit and quadruple the performance.

The dirt-poor cowboy had suddenly become the golden boy of the electronics industry, and he'd passed it on to his son right out of college. No, he wasn't old money. He was new money, and a rough-edged cowboy, who just happened to be as good in the boardroom as he was on the back of a horse.

Luckily, he enjoyed both things. So, the money came and J.T. never looked back.

"Stranger things have happened," Jack said. "Like me finding love. Can you believe it? And Patrick was the one to see it first." He chuckled softly. "That kid...he's something."

"My godson *is* very special," J.T. said. "So who's the lucky girl?"

"Her name is Sandi. But I'm the lucky one." He went on without a pause. "I need to ask you something."

"I don't give advice on marriage," he said as the elevator slowed.

"I don't need any. What I need is for you to be one of my best men."

"*One* of your best men?" he asked with a grin as the floor indicator dinged softly. "Pardner, what are you talking about?"

"You and Dylan are going to be my best men. Whitney and Steffi are the matrons of honor. Sandi has it all figured out. Partick's the ring bearer. The wedding's two weeks from today, at twilight, on the beach below the old hotel by the plaza in Montgomery Beach."

The last two words made no sense at all. "What are you talking about? Montgomery Beach?"

"I met Sandi here, fell in love here, and Sandi and Patrick and myself are going to make our life here. That's why it's going to start here."

The idea of heading back to Montgomery Beach, California, didn't sit well with him. He hadn't been there for eight years, and he wasn't in a hurry to go back. Besides, now that he thought about it, this merger wasn't going to let him get away from Dallas any time soon. The doors slid open as he said, "I'm sorry, but you got me at a bad time. Two weeks is not doable for me."

"What?"

"Work, this merger." He stepped into the cavernous parking garage that was almost deserted. "I can't delegate most of it. If I could, I would, but it's just bad timing."

"The way it was for Dylan's wedding?"

He stopped by the doors as they slid shut behind him. "Hey, I feel bad about that, too, and I told him I'd make it up to him later. But it couldn't be helped."

"If you can't take care of that merger in two weeks' time, you and your company are in deep horse pucky."

"It won't be the first time I've shoveled muck, and it won't be the last."

"You can leave it for a day if you have to."

"I'm in London, in case you forgot." A world away from Montgomery Beach.

"Surely you've heard of the Concorde?"

J.T. grimaced as he turned to head for the hunter green Jaguar they'd leased for him. "Jack, you don't—"

"Oh, but I do," he said, cutting him off. "I get it."

"You get what?"

"Why you're hedging all over the place, and why you don't want to come back here."

He strode toward the car, the heels of his boots clicking eerily in the underground parking space as he tried to kill a nudge of frustration with Jack. "Okay, since I've explained it to you, you tell me your version of me being stuck here with tons of work.''

"Let's put it this way, Dylan's the only Montgomery coming to the wedding.''

Tension tightened in his shoulders and started a headache at his temples, a sudden reaction that came from nowhere. ''And the point of this announcement is?'' he asked as he neared the car.

"She won't be there, J.T.''

He stopped at the driver's door, his hand on the cold metal of the handle. But he didn't open it. ''What?''

"Her mother's barely through her year of mourning for her father, and Candice is on a cruise somewhere in the Caribbean. I don't even know when she's due back.''

"Thanks for the update,'' he drawled, jerking the car door open and slipping into the leather interior. He pushed the keys into the ignition, but didn't start the car. Instead, he sank back in the soft seat and slipped off his Stetson, tossing it onto the passenger seat. As he raked his fingers through his dark brown hair, he added, ''What are you, a social commentator on the Montgomerys now?''

"Just letting you know. Now you don't have a reason for not coming.''

He exhaled, fighting even visualizing Candice. He never revisited past mistakes. Never. ''That wasn't my reason, to begin with.''

"Bull,'' Jack said tensely. ''Tell it to someone who believes it. You're still mad as hell about what happened. The way the family dismissed you and controlled her.''

He didn't know if he was still mad, but he knew

that just the thought of the Montgomerys made him
wonder how Dylan could have come out of a family
like that. Solid, good-hearted, with no airs, the guy
was a great friend and the exact opposite of his parents and of Candice.

He glanced in the rearview mirror at hazel eyes
under heavy eyebrows. Maybe there was still some
anger. The only residue of that mistake eight years
ago. No cowboy for their princess, a princess who
wouldn't stand up to the king.

"That's over and done, water under the bridge,"
J.T. said.

"Then I guess it won't hurt to tell you that she's
engaged."

The words were said, and they meant nothing to
him at first. Candice was engaged. He sat up a bit,
gripping the steering wheel with his free hand. Of
course he'd known that Candice would marry sooner
or later, in fact, he was surprised she wasn't already
by now. Surely some man would see her and want
her and love her. Hell, he'd been there, done that
and knew he couldn't be the only one, even if he
was the first.

"So, she's engaged?" he asked.

"Just got engaged, and they headed off for his
parents' house on some island in the Caribbean."

"She found someone suitable, I take it?"

"Very suitable. Mark Forester, old money, Palm
Beach, and her father took him on as a sort of pro-
tégé and groomed him to be second in command to
Dylan."

Old money and a Montgomery protégé. His middle knotted. Just what her father had wanted for

Candice. "So, is he going to take the Montgomery name, too?"

"Sarcasm doesn't become you, J.T.," Jack muttered.

"Sorry, it just slipped out."

"Don't apologize, just come to my wedding. I need you here. Let Davis take over for a day. How much damage can your assistant do in twenty-four hours?"

He could get married, make love passionately and find out it was all a mistake in twenty-four hours, J.T. thought with a tinge of uncharacteristic bitterness. That made no sense to him. The Montgomerys were nothing to him. Whether they were there or not didn't matter. And Davis sure as hell could hold down the fort for a day or two.

"Okay, you win." He started the engine and felt the power of the car roar to life. "I'll try to get there."

"That's great."

As he drove up the concrete ramp and out onto the midnight London streets, he said, "I've got to meet any woman who got you to even think about love, let alone marriage." He slowed at a signal and fingered the steering wheel. "Give me details."

"You'll have to wear a tux. I know that's overkill for you, but take heart in the fact that you don't have to wear any shoes."

"Barefoot in a tux? You all are very original," he drawled, turning up the street to his hotel, which was near Hanover Square. "I'll get this business going, then get Davis to take over for a few days. I'll let you know when to expect me."

J.T. approached the valet entrance for the hotel

and braked to a stop by the red-uniformed attendant as Jack said, "Have your tailor contact Karl Delaney at his tailor shop."

"Sure," he said, getting out and letting the attendant take the car while he headed into the hotel. He saw the elevators, but didn't head for them. Instead, he went into the pub area while Jack told him more details. He slipped onto a dark wood and leather stool, then motioned for a drink.

"Anything else I should know, such as what you want for a wedding gift?" he asked into the phone.

Jack was talking, saying something about Sandi being registered, but he didn't catch any more of what was being said. He had a startling flash of the past. A willowy blonde, with the bluest eyes, smiling up at him. God, it made his breath catch in his chest, and he took a quick drink, letting the fire of the alcohol break up whatever had happened to him.

After eight long years, that image of a nineteen-year-old Candice was still as clear as if he'd just seen her. That shook him, after he'd forgotten it all this time. He'd closed the door when he left, and he could almost feel it starting to open. That made him vaguely uneasy, and he drank the rest of his drink in one swallow.

"Are you still there?" Jack asked on the other end of the line.

"Yeah, sure, I'm listening."

"Call me when you know when you'll get here. Patrick is dying to see you again."

"Tell the little hoodlum his godfather will be seeing him soon," he said.

"Why not bring a date, maybe that model?"

J.T. fingered the cool condensation on the smooth side of his drink glass. "I'll ask her."

"Great. See you when you get here," Jack said, then the line went dead.

J.T. flipped his phone shut and slipped it into the inner pocket of his jacket. Yes, he'd ask Vonya to go. Seeing her would be a good idea. He'd been gone too long. And she'd love an excuse for a party, if she could create a hole in her schedule.

Dark and beautiful, it was no wonder she was one of the top models in the business. Chocolate-brown eyes that could smolder, fueling a man's fantasies. One touch could take a man's mind off a nuclear explosion in his own backyard. He started to smile at that, but the expression froze when a delicate blonde blotted out Vonya's sultry image. Blue eyes drowned out brown, and a golden tan dominated a deep, coppery tan.

"Damn it," he muttered.

Candice was his past, and even though he was going to Montgomery Beach, he wasn't going to revisit that past. He was older, wiser, and Candice Montgomery was nothing to him.

Chapter One

Montgomery Beach, California
Two weeks later

"I had everything planned, everything, then at the last minute, everything changes." Sandi Galloway paced back and forth in the dressing room off the ballroom in the old, Spanish-style hotel, looking beautiful in her wedding dress. But her face was filled with anxiety. "I wanted it to be perfect, just perfect. Then that damn hurricane messed up everything."

Candice Montgomery looked in the floor-length mirrors in the room, and had to bite her lip to keep from reminding Sandi that she couldn't blame this dress on any hurricane. The dress was actually two pieces, done in a shimmering gold material, with a skimpy, sleeveless, bare-midriff top with scalloped hemming that barely covered her breasts and left her stomach exposed.

And the skirt... She smoothed anxiously at the shimmering material that clung to her like a second skin, and had a slit up the right side almost past her thigh. Even the shoes were gold, with three-inch heels.

She was in the wedding by default, and had, actually, only known about it for a couple of hours. She'd stepped off the plane from the Caribbean and found Karl Delaney waiting for her with the news that Dylan and Whitney were grounded and Sandi wanted her to take Whitney's place.

"As long as Dylan and Whitney are safe wherever they are, things aren't too bad." She had talked to Sandi for probably five minutes tops since being whisked to the hotel and to the fitting for the dress. Now Sandi was in her gown, pacing the dressing area, barely pausing from time to time to check on herself in the mirrors.

"I don't know how to thank you, Candice, stepping in for Whitney like this. And the dress fits you perfectly. Karl is a genius, isn't he?"

"Did Whitney ever see this dress?" she asked, twisting right and left while she tugged at the top, vainly trying to get it to cover a bit more of her stomach.

"No, she didn't." Sandi stopped pacing long enough to study Candice. "I have to say, it's stunning on you. You're tall, have a perfect figure and your hair is blond enough to pick up the gold highlights." She came around to stand halfway between Candice and the mirrors. "If I didn't like you so much, I'd hate you," she said with a grin.

Candice felt the same way about Sandi. She was an odd mixture of fun and sanity, a person who could put you in your place with a word, though that word wouldn't be meant in a mean spirit. Right now she looked stunning in a very traditional wedding dress, white and beautiful, and she looked...well, radiant. An old saying about a bride, but Sandi really did look radiant. There was something inside her that just glowed. "It shows half of..." She glanced down at bare stomach. "Did you have to go this far?"

Sandi lightly slapped at Candice's hand when she started tugging at the top again. "Leave it alone. You look terrific."

"It's almost time," a woman's voice announced. A gray-haired lady, whom Candice thought was an aunt or someone related to Sandi and her sister, Steffi, popped into the dressing area. Dressed all in purple, the woman glowed, but in a different way. "Mr. Delaney has the men already done, and they're on their way to the beach. He says that you three..." She glanced past Sandi and Candice. "Where did Steffi get to?"

"Steffi is right here," someone said from behind, and Candice turned as Sandi's sister hurried into the room. Candice hadn't seen Steffi since Dylan's wedding, and now she was in *the* dress, gold and glittery and with the bare midriff and side slit, but Steffi gave it a confident flare that Candice knew she didn't have. Steffi wore it easily, as if she actually enjoyed it.

"I'm here and dressed." Steffi posed with both hands over her head, fingers touching. "And what a dress." She spun around and grinned. "I thought Greg was going to make me late when he saw me in it."

"Don't even talk about being late," Sandi said. "This has to be absolutely perfect."

"Of course, of course," Steffi said, coming over

to where Sandi and Candice were standing. "And it's going to be. Mine was, now it's your turn." She smiled at Candice. "Okay, show me the rock."

Candice didn't understand until Steffi reached for her left hand and lifted it. "Oh, the ring. I don't have it."

Steffi let go of her hand. "You don't have it? You two didn't break up, did you? I didn't see him downstairs."

"No, no, not at all. Mark got the ring in Portugal, and it's a bit too big. He's having it sized for me. And he promised he'd be here for the ceremony."

"So, when is the big day for you and Mark?"

Candice hadn't even thought about a date yet. Just getting used to the idea of being engaged, and trying to talk her mother and his parents out of a ton of parties and celebrations, had taken up most of her time in the past two weeks. "We haven't decided yet. Probably next year."

Sandi stood in front of the mirror, staring at herself intently. "If Jack and I had waited any longer, I don't think I could have survived." She met Candice's gaze in the mirrored reflection. "How can you wait that long?"

"There's so much to do," Candice said. "And we both work, so it made sense to wait for a while."

"I understand. You want everything to be perfect. I mean, we thought of eloping, but just couldn't do that to everyone." She fussed with her low neckline. "Maybe we should have and all this craziness wouldn't be happening. But this is forever. We wanted it to be just right."

Candice looked away from Sandi to herself in the mirror. A tall, slender woman, with a cap of blond

hair and blue eyes, wearing a blatantly sexy dress.
But for a flashing moment she was jarred by the
overlapping image of a young girl—a girl she used
to be eight years ago—with longer hair, jeans and a
crop-top sweater. A crazy girl, running away to
marry a man she thought she loved, but a man she
never really knew.

That was what crazy was all about. And it hadn't
been forever. She shrugged sharply and forced herself to shut out a past she'd deliberately relegated to
a region of forgetfulness. She didn't want to think
about it. There was no point. It didn't even feel real
anymore, more like a dream that she'd awaken from
to her real life still in progress. J. T. Watson wasn't
part of that real life. Even when she'd seen pictures
of him and some model in the paper, she'd found
herself looking at a stranger, a man who had no
substance for her now.

"I'm sure you'll never regret not eloping," she
said.

"To be honest, I'll take Jack any way I can get
him," Sandi said with a girlish giggle. "Any way
at all."

"And I'm sure you will," Steffi said.

The three women laughed at that, easing the tension surrounding them. Then Sandi was in motion
again, heading out of the dressing area only to return
moments later carrying flowers strewn with glittery
gold ribbons. She handed Steffi some, then turned
to offer Candice a bouquet of roses and baby's
breath.

"Thank you both for being here," she said. "And
thank you, Candice, for filling in at the last moment.
It's as if it was meant to be this way."

"I'm glad to be here," Candice said, actually starting to feel good about being here, after all.

"It's time," someone announced, and all three women turned to see Karl Delaney in the doorway. The tall man with silvery hair came closer, stopping by Candice. Karl was more than a well-known tailor. To the Montgomerys he was a long-time friend and confidant. His blue eyes crinkled with a smile that twitched at his neatly trimmed gray mustache as he touched Candice lightly on the shoulder. "And I shall be very interested in seeing how your mother reacts to your dress," he said, his deep voice touched with a trace of a Russian accent.

"I thought Mother wasn't coming," Candice said, fully expecting her mother to beg off and stay home alone. For the past year, she'd stayed close to the house, seldom going out. Mourning was serious business for her mother, and the year was barely up.

"I just left her downstairs," Karl said. "And she looks lovely."

"That's wonderful that she could come," Sandi said.

Candice wasn't so sure. The old joke about her fainting wouldn't be too far off when she saw this dress. Although Grace Montgomery never fainted. It wasn't the thing to do. But she never had any trouble showing her disapproval in subtle ways. Disapproval about clothing, and especially about people.

Candice loved her mother a great deal, but something in her knew that Grace was lacking something...something Candice had never been able to put her finger on. But she'd felt it from time to time. An incident from the past was there, something she could have sworn she'd forgotten, but it was there as clearly as if it had just been yesterday.

"Candice, you know that we like J.T., that he's a good friend to Dylan, but the man..." Her mother had shrugged her petite shoulders and given that half smile meant to soften what she was about to say. *"He's very...different, don't you think?"*

Candice had known exactly what her mother meant, even though she'd been only eighteen at the time. J.T. was fine for a friend, but nothing more. And right then, he hadn't been anything more. But her mother's opinion had been there, unwavering, and unquestioned. Even the next year, when J.T. came back to the estate at college graduation, her mother hadn't changed her opinion. It was Candice who had changed.

Candice came back to the present with a jolt, a shade shaken that that particular memory had come to her at all. She'd been so determined to forget the past, to put it behind her. Then the image was there. She looked around, blaming the memory on the wedding. One wedding reminding her of another. But that didn't make it right, and she vowed to keep thoughts of J.T. banished.

"Your mother will smile and nod," Karl was saying, "and will be a lady at any cost."

Candice frowned slightly at him, at the touch of tension in his voice. She didn't understand that, either. But before she could say or do anything, it was gone and he was smiling again. "You are all so beautiful. This is truly going to be a wonderful experience. A long-overdue experience," he said. He held out an arm in an old-world manner to Candice. "Come, it is time to go down to the beach."

Candice hesitated, then slipped her hand into the crook of Karl's arm. "How are the men holding up?" Sandi asked as they walked into a ballroom done in gold, silver and crystal.

"Oh, just fine. Everything is ready. The music. The lights. The minister. It is all in place." He glanced at her as they walked across the ballroom to the open doors and the terrace. "I did not mean to upset you by commenting about your mother," he said in a lower voice.

"No, you didn't. I was just surprised that she decided to come."

"She is a woman of many surprises," he said softly as they got to the doors and stepped out into the softness of twilight.

Her mother? A woman of surprises? Now *that* surprised her. Almost as much as Karl saying it. "I'm surprised to be in this wedding," she said. "What a chain of coincidences."

He patted her hand softly. "One thing you will learn as you get older, Candice, is that nothing in life ever happens by chance."

"You don't believe in luck?" she asked as they approached the stairs that led down to the beach.

"Yes, I believe in luck." Karl stopped with her near the top of the stairs and his hand over hers pressed down slightly. His blue eyes held no humor, only a deep intensity that she didn't understand. "I also believe that luck is what we make of it," he murmured, then he stepped back a bit as the gray-haired lady began arranging the wedding party for the procession down the stairs.

Karl stood off to one side as the flower girl was brought in to start at the top of the stairs, then Candice, Steffi, and finally, the bride. Music from the beach below drifted up to the waiting party, and a tangible excitement was in the soft evening air.

Even Karl seems a bit nervous, she thought as she glanced at the man. He caught her gaze, smiled at her, then quietly came over to her. "Good luck," he murmured, then unexpectedly leaned toward her and kissed her lightly on the cheek.

Karl had been around as long as she could remember, a person who had always been in her life one way or another, but mostly through her best friend, Whitney. He had hugged her, patted her hand, offered her his arm, but he had never kissed her until now. And why pay her all this attention, when Sandi was the bride? Shouldn't he be kissing Sandi and wishing *her* good luck?

Oddly, it seemed right the way he'd done it. She looked at him, his blue eyes narrowed on her as he drew back and murmured, "Whitney would be proud to have you take her place. Now, get on with it." Then he was gone and the flower girl started down the stairs.

Candice turned, stepped out of her shoes when the others did and straightened her shoulders. When she felt her top ride up a bit, she pulled the bouquet to cover her middle, then heard the strains of the wedding march drifting up from the beach below. The music was lovely and almost ethereal, played by a string quartet as the colors of twilight spread across the sky. She started after the flower girl, the smooth wood of the steps cool under her bare feet.

It was perfect. The way a wedding should be perfect. Not like in some tacky wedding chapel in Nevada, with pink-satin benches and a justice of the

peace dressed all in white. And the music, tinny and
hollow, coming out of a small cassette player. J.T.,
there, so close she'd felt as if she just had to move
a bit closer and he would have absorbed her. She
would have been part of him....

She trembled as she kept going, and images of
the past persisted, drawn to her, no doubt, because
of the wedding going on. Yet Dylan's wedding
hadn't done this to her. It hadn't brought this pain,
along with images she'd thought long gone. She
took another breath, ignoring the way her stomach
was clenching, and took the stairs slowly and carefully. Enough, she thought, hating the way the past
never really went away, even when it was supposed
to have been erased, as if it had never been.

That's what an annulment was, after all. An era-
sure of what had been, leaving a blank space where
once there had been a past. An impulsive marriage.
Gone. She held more tightly to the flowers. Damn
it, J.T. wasn't a part of her life. He'd barely touched
it eight years ago, and had disappeared as if he had
never been. Maybe he'd been an illusion, after all.

As she reached the final step, she looked up at
the wedding circle. Jack and Patrick were by a
bower of roses entwined with gold, the minister to
one side and behind them. Maybe a hundred guests
were grouped on the sand, framed by soft lights
strung overhead. Tuxedos were everywhere. Elegant
dresses and bare feet. A smile started to play at her
lips, growing as she glanced to Jack's left to Patrick.

The boy, a miniature version of his dad, was grinning from ear to ear, obviously thrilled by everything. Actually, she was starting to enjoy this. The
evening, the sense of joy in the air, being here. She

glanced away from Patrick as she stepped onto the silky warmth of the sand, intending to find Mark among the guests. It was then that she realized there was another man standing at the front, a lean man in a perfectly cut tuxedo.

Her smile grew when she thought that Dylan must have made it back, but that couldn't be, since he was stranded with Whitney. Besides, this man was taller than Dylan. Darker than Dylan. More tanned than Dylan. She'd heard of a person's heart jumping into their throat, but she'd never believed it could actually happen until that moment when she realized J.T. was standing there.

She stumbled slightly, stopping as eight years were wiped away as if they had never been. J.T. was there, a reality in a tuxedo with the heavens splashed with twilight behind him. Even in the soft glow of the twinkling lights, the man was painfully there, watching the flower girl throw rose petals on the sand. His dark hair was longer, brushed back from a clean-shaven face that looked older and rougher with angles and planes and a slash of dark eyebrows.

The fine tailoring of the tuxedo couldn't wipe away lingering traces of a certain roughness about him, while, at the same time, it defined his whipcord leanness. For a moment she thought she'd gone mad, that the spell this wedding had cast on her in the most perverse way was trying to bring back a wedding that never should have been. Then she felt Steffi behind her, touching her in the small of her back as she whispered, "Not here. Over there." And she nudged her toward the bower and the men.

As if on cue, J.T. looked up, and their eyes met. Hazel met blue, and the jolt in Candice all but took

her breath away. It gave her a certain satisfaction
that she saw her own shock echoed in his face, then
she grabbed at reality. This was crazy, ridiculous.
So what if J.T. was here? It meant nothing at all.
This wasn't eight years ago, and she wasn't a foolish
kid taken in by tight jeans, a rough voice and a way
of looking at her that could melt her bones.

She grabbed at control, drawing it around her like
a security blanket. She stood straighter, broke their
eye contact and took steps forward. She concentrated on everything else but the man to her left. She
smiled at Jack, slipped into her place opposite the
men and turned to watch Steffi slip in beside her
just as Sandi came down the steps.

No one had said he'd be in the wedding, but then
again, she'd never asked. It had been such a whirlwind, from the moment Karl met the plane, through
the dress fitting, dressing and getting down here, that
there had been little time to discuss anything. But
this was okay. She was breathing normally, and she
could feel her heart steadying. It was okay. It didn't
mean a thing that J.T. was here. Nothing.

J.T. STOOD BY JACK—an obviously happy and nervous Jack—and Patrick, who was drawing circles in
the sand with his bare toes. He smiled at Vonya
standing with the other guests, a vision in shimmering black, enjoying the buzz she'd caused when they
arrived. She didn't go anywhere unnoticed, but she
liked that and he liked her. She was fun, and she
didn't demand anything of him beyond the moment.
A workable relationship.

He heard the music swell, then turned to see the
tiny flower girl coming down the stairs, a beautiful,

angelic child, methodically scattering rose petals. It wasn't until the little girl was on the sand, crossing to where the men stood, that he actually looked past her.

He stared at a woman in a golden gown, the last rays of the sunlight catching at the glittery material and reflecting the richness in her blond hair. Suddenly, his past was far from dead.

Somewhere to his right, Jack was murmuring, ''I swear I didn't know. Karl Delaney just said he would take care of Whitney's replacement.''

J.T. stared at Candice, not bothering to hide his shock as she looked directly at him. God, it was like going back in time, her all golden and beautiful, her hair shorter, a cap of paleness that framed a startlingly beautiful face. Finely boned, dominated by eyes widened by shock. Eyes that had brought fire with one glance.

Whatever had been there eight years ago when they'd looked at each other was still there, as potent as it had been; yet as suddenly as he sensed it, it was gone. She withdrew, controlled and cool, walking to her spot across from him. She never looked at him again, choosing to turn toward the stairs to watch Sandi's approach.

Her blue eyes were blurred softly by the low light, and the sweep of her throat was tempting. Very tempting. He pressed his feet into the sand and wished he could look away. But there was something there, almost the same fascination a person has with a sore tooth. Testing it, touching it, yet knowing it was only going to get more painful. He couldn't make himself breathe without thinking about each time he inhaled and exhaled.

She stood by Steffi, turned to watch Sandi, but all he saw was how beautiful she looked with the night forming behind her. Damn it, nothing had changed. She drew him in in a physical way that defied explanation. Maybe there never had been one. But it was still there. And it was still just as ridiculous.

For a moment he couldn't remember why he'd ever let her go, why he hadn't stopped her when she'd walked away from him to get on the plane to go back to this place. Then she turned slightly, her eyes flicking to his, and he knew. There was nothing there. The Montgomery veil was in place. And he remembered. The bitterness that still touched his tongue was surprisingly pungent. He remembered and it eased his breathing and slowed his heart rate. Oh, yes, he remembered.

He turned from Candice and the past, slipped one hand into his pocket and looked at Sandi, just taking her place by Jack, her hand lifting to rest in her future husband's hand. His fingers touched something in his pocket, a piece of paper, but he barely noticed it as he fought off the past and concentrated on the present and the reason he was here.

But in a single heartbeat it was there, a flashing memory of his reality eight years ago. Candice, him, that moment when he knew he'd wanted her forever. The moment when he'd touched her, inhaled her essence, that blur of wanting and passion that burned far too brightly to survive. Twenty-four hours had been the life span. Twenty-four mad, insane, fiery hours of completion that he'd never known before...or since. Bitterness rose again at the magnitude of his mistake, and he put both hands at his sides, making sure not to ball them into fists.

Actually, he was relieved to feel the tinge of anger, anger he could focus on Candice and her family. He watched Jack and Sandi, the minister smiling and saying words that he couldn't quite make out. It was a blur—the night, the vows, then the kiss—and he thought he had it all together. He'd get through this. Keep his distance from Candice, and it wouldn't mean a thing. Nothing.

That thought lasted until the minister said, "Ladies and gentlemen, I would like to present Mr. and Mrs. Jack O'Connor."

Patrick was jumping up and down, yelling with delight, "I've got a mom. I've got a mom!"

Then Jack was picking up Sandi and spinning her around in a circle while Patrick laughed and danced around them. J.T. was aware of Jack moving, going toward the water, but he was looking at Candice, who was watching the bride and groom, too. She lifted her chin slightly, a smile playing on her full lips that made him ache, a sensation he couldn't control, and that brought more anger. Directed at himself.

She wasn't even aware of him now, not beyond that first shock, and now she was giving Patrick high fives, her laughter mingling with the other guests'. There was one glance in his direction, then her slender shoulder turned ever so slightly, effectively shutting him out. A deliberate Montgomery trick. Cut off the infidel. Don't even give him a chance to intrude.

"*He's a cowboy,*" the old man had said more than once. "*Beans and franks and cows.*" Then that laugh that J.T. had hated so much.

He turned from the sight of Candice, and Vonya

was there, smiling and throwing herself into his arms. "It is too wonderful," she gushed in that husky voice. "Weddings and love and romance." Then she drew back. "What a wonderful idea to invite me."

He slipped his arm around her waist and let her presence blot out anything else. She was good medicine right then, very good medicine. And he kissed her lightly and quickly, before drawing back when he heard Sandi squeal.

"Oh, no," Vonya said, twining her arm in his. "Can you believe what he's doing to her?"

He turned to see Jack with Sandi still in his arms, calf deep in the waves, the water lapping around his legs. Sandi was squealing, "Jack!" but he went deeper, then smiled as he let her fall into the water. But she had a hold on him, pulling him down with her. The guests laughed and clapped, while Jack and Sandi got doused in the surf.

Vonya let go of J.T. and hurried toward the ring of guests by the water's edge, and it was then that J.T. felt someone brush past him. The air was touched by a subtle fragrance that brought back the past...then Candice was there, heading away from him. A slight contact made through the jacket of his tuxedo jolted him, and he swiped at the contact point to kill the sensation.

As he watched her walking toward the water's edge with the others, he admitted that whatever anger there was, she was still sexy. She still could make him think things he had no business thinking. Then she was side by side with Vonya. Light and dark. The past and the present.

He went toward the two women.

Chapter Two

Candice hurried past J.T., though not agilely enough to avoid bumping arms with him. The jolt from the contact almost made her gasp, but she kept going, keeping her back to him, getting distance from him. She was near the water, felt the cool dampness on her bare feet and laughed with the others as Jack and Sandi struggled to get out of the water.

There was applause and laughter. Patrick wading in after them. And she almost forgot about J.T. somewhere behind her. At least she did until he was there, by her shoulder, and she could feel his body heat on the bare skin of her shoulder and arm. Despite the heat, she trembled when he said in a low voice, "Anyone for a swim?"

"I don't..." Her voice trailed off as she turned and realized that he wasn't talking to her. Why had she thought he would be? He was talking to a stunning, dark-haired woman, who was slender as a reed and just a few feet from her.

A woman who slipped her arm into his as if she'd been doing it forever, who smiled at him, showing absolutely perfect white teeth. The model. The one the papers had called his "filly." "Why, sweetheart, whatever are you suggesting?'' she said in a husky voice that dripped with intimacy.

Candice took a step back, the sense of being a voyeur so strong that she had to keep herself from turning and running. Of course J.T. was with the woman. Of course. She touched her tongue to her cold lips. He'd been with lots of women, she was sure. She'd seen the pictures, read the snippets in the gossip columns. But they had never seemed real to her, somehow there had been no connection at all. Not until now.

She would have moved back farther, but at that moment, J.T. turned and was looking right at her. ''Candice,'' he said, her name sounding odd on his lips. ''It's been a long time.''

She stood very still, a bit surprised when she found her voice and it sounded almost normal. ''Yes, it has been.''

''I didn't know you'd be here,'' he said.

''That goes both ways. No one told me you were in the wedding party.''

''You didn't figure that since Jack and I were best friends, I just might be here?''

''You weren't here for Dylan,'' she said, wishing she could turn her back on him and walk away. That she could stop being aware of the way the woman with him was moving closer to him, pressing her cheek to his shoulder. But her breeding was too deep to acknowledge any of that. No, she'd make small talk, be polite, and leave as soon as she could.

''I was busy with work,'' he said, all but ignoring the model as she started slowly feathering her fingertips up and down his arm. The silver polish caught in the light, and Candice could have sworn the woman had a ruby studded in the nail of her forefinger.

"Of course," Candice said, hearing the growing tightness in her voice.

"I knew you'd understand that," he said.

She didn't know how long she could stand this meaningless conversation or the way the woman was pawing J.T. in public, so she decided to break it up with manners, smiling at the woman with him. "You have to forgive J.T. Either he's dealing with cowboys who don't have a clue about manners, or he's dealing with businessmen who don't care about manners. I'm Candice."

The woman kept her hold on J.T. "I'm Vonya," she said to Candice, then turned to J.T. "And I'm hungry. You have to come up to the terrace with me and keep me from devouring the food. Let's go."

J.T. was looking at Candice, she could feel his eyes on her while she watched Vonya, and she almost willed him to leave. But whatever she wanted didn't affect J.T. at all. "You go ahead, darlin'," he said without looking at Vonya. "I'll be up soon."

The dark-haired woman hesitated. "Okay, but don't be too long," she said, brushing a kiss across his cheek, leaving just a hint of deep magenta lipstick before she started across the sand.

Candice watched her move, then glanced at J.T. "A good friend?"

"A friend."

"You should have gone with her."

"I will in a few minutes."

"She might need you to wrestle a celery stalk out of her hand before she binges on it."

Incredibly, that made him smile, an expression

she'd entirely forgotten. She wished she hadn't seen it again, not the way his eyes crinkled or the way it showed the suggestion of a single dimple on one cheek.

"Whoa, who would have thought a Montgomery could be catty?"

A suffocating sensation was making it difficult for her to breathe. "Who would have thought you'd be with…" She bit her lip. "That sort of woman."

"*That* sort of woman?" he asked, the smile thankfully dying with each word.

"She seems high-maintenance," she said, words coming out of her mouth that she hadn't consciously thought about before uttering. "I know how much you hate complications and demands."

"You're right, I'm not good at any of that." His hazel eyes were intent on her. "I like things simple and direct. And Vonya, despite appearances, is very simple and direct."

"Sure, and a dog lays eggs."

He stared at her, then suddenly laughed, really laughed, an explosion of humor that rocked her. "Darlin', where on earth did that come from?"

She didn't have a clue, not any more than she understood why she was standing here verbally sparring with J.T. "If there's nothing else," she murmured.

But he didn't move. "Nice dress," he murmured back.

Unexpectedly, he reached out, lightly brushing the tip of his forefinger along her bare arm. The slight roughness belied his status as CEO of an international company. She knew if she looked at his hands, there would be calluses from working on the ranch. Calluses that she remembered from his touch long ago. She trembled, jerking back from the contact.

"It was supposed to be for Whitney."

She tensed when his gaze flicked over her, lingering on her bare middle. "Fits you perfectly," he drawled, his Texas accent even more pronounced.

A hand touched her shoulder from behind, and she jumped at the contact. Then she turned and Mark was there, smiling and so very solid and real. "Candice," he said. "I just got here. Business calls just wouldn't stop."

Mark wasn't big on public displays, but that didn't stop Candice from moving closer and hugging him around the waist. "At least you're here," she said, finally able to take a breath that wasn't constricted.

She felt him stiffen slightly, then his arm went around her and she eased back, but stayed in his hold as she glanced back at J.T. She didn't miss the way he flicked his gaze over Mark. At six foot two, with blond hair, a year-round tan and classic features, Mark was a good-looking man. He was also one of the strengths behind the family-owned business, bright, engaging and dependable.

"I'm no expert on manners," J.T. said, looking at Candice. "But I think an introduction is in order."

"J. T. Watson, Mark Forester," she said somewhat reluctantly.

"Oh, yes, of course." J.T. put out his hand to the other man. "I should have known."

"Have we met?" Mark asked as he shook hands

with J.T., then drew back to hold Candice a bit more tightly.

"No, but I've heard about you." He glanced at Candice, his eyes unreadable. "Jack says you're engaged." He glanced at her hand. "But I didn't see a ring."

Mark patted his breast pocket. "I've got it right here," he said.

J.T. glanced at Mark. "A new tradition, the soon-to-be groom carries the ring around with him?"

Mark laughed at that. "No, just a sizing problem. But it's fixed."

"So, when's the big day?"

Mark's hold on her tightened a bit more, holding her to him. "The sooner the better, but Candice wants to wait a while. Probably next spring."

J.T. lifted one eyebrow in her direction. "Oh, you're not rushing into anything."

She found her own hold on Mark's waist tightening as she realized what J.T. was doing. She hated sarcasm, even when it was veiled by an innocuous comment. "No, I'm not. That never works out. You can get yourself in a real mess by rushing."

J.T. shrugged. "There's always divorce or...annulment."

He said it so casually that it shook her. Then Mark was speaking, and his words only added to her discomfort. "No, we're doing this once. Period. And we're doing it right." He pressed his lips to her forehead. "Isn't that right, Candice?"

"Yes...right," she whispered.

She'd never told anyone but Whitney about the fiasco with J.T. She'd never intended to. The annulment had washed it away. But now she knew that if she told one other person, it had to be Mark. She could feel a sense of pressure building that had never existed until this moment.

Mark's hold on her eased a bit. "Are you the same J. T. Watson who's working with Vortox?"

"That's me."

"No wonder your name sounded so familiar. But I thought you were off in Europe negotiating and—"

J.T. cut him off. "That's me, and I'm obviously here, but let's not talk business tonight." He looked at Candice. "Not when you have such a beautiful woman with you."

Mark laughed. "You're right." He was holding Candice tightly again. "No business talk. There are a lot better things to do than talk."

Candice could see J.T.'s expression tighten, but he simply said, "Smart man," and with a nod walked away.

Candice had a sudden flash of an image of J.T. at the airport in Nevada. She'd been boarding the plane and had looked back just once. Once was all she needed to see J.T. walking away. He'd never looked back.

She felt Mark by her, then looked up at him. Mark would never do that. He would have fought for her, gone after her, tried to talk her into staying. But not J.T.

She turned in Mark's arms and stated the truth, "I'm so glad you made it, late or not."

"So am I," he said, so close his breath brushed her skin with much-needed warmth. "I wouldn't have wanted to miss seeing you in that dress."

She laughed a bit unsteadily. "It's quite a dress."

"Quite a lady in that dress." He hesitated, then said, "And a lady I really want to marry." Before she could say anything, he continued, "I know, you're thinking about it, but can't we do this faster?" He pulled her around to face him, then hugged her, almost taking her breath away. "Remember, I'm human, and I can't wait too long."

She was enveloped in his arms, arms that didn't belong to J.T. Listening to a heart beat against her cheek that wasn't J.T.'s. She hated herself for even making comparisons where Mark and J.T. were concerned.

Then Mark was holding her back, his hands framing her face. "What about it?" He smiled at her. "Why not get married in a few months... How about Labor Day weekend? Enough time for our parents to do it up right, and yet it's not that far away. Just the summer. How about it?"

As she stared up at him, she didn't know why there was moisture on her lashes. He wanted to marry her because he loved her. She wasn't worried about what would happen after they said their vows, how her life would change. She wasn't scared that he might walk away.

She should be happy, not confused and unsteady. "Oh, Mark, I just..."

He smiled, a shaky expression. "Just say, 'Mark, I love you and I'll marry you anywhere, any time,' and let's do it."

The tears did come then, but the words wouldn't. Simple words, but words she'd never been able to say to any man. And the only time she'd even thought about saying, "I love you," it hadn't been real, making her eternally grateful that she'd never uttered the words.

Mark let her go. Then she realized what he was doing. He reached into his pocket and took out the ring, an intricate rose fashioned in platinum, with a single perfect diamond in its center. He lifted her hand, slipped the ring on her finger and whispered, "I do."

She must love him. She surely liked him, and he was touching her with what he was doing. He was comforting, not making her crazy. She almost laughed at that, but the sound came out as a small sob, and she leaned forward to bury her face in his chest.

But not before she had a glimpse of J.T. at the water's edge, standing alone, staring at her and Mark.

Damn J.T. and damn herself for letting him still get to her. She wasn't going to let him make her crazy, not now. She wasn't going to let him affect her when she was with Mark.

She could put him out of her life for good, and she knew how to do it. The sooner the better. When she moved back and J.T. was gone, she managed an unsteady smile. Then she said the words that were meant to put J.T. and her past behind her once and for all.

"Yes, yes, Labor Day. I'll marry you then."

As J.T. TURNED from the sight of Mark slipping the ring on Candice's finger, he thought about the ring he'd given her. He didn't even know where it had gone. There was a memory of her taking it off, but that was it. A simple gold band he'd bought at the

jeweler's near the chapel. A hundred dollars. Not a
great loss, he conceded, no matter what happened to
it.

He almost ran into Jack, and barely stopped before impact. The groom was wet, his tuxedo ruined,
and he had a very white towel draped around his
neck. He held both ends with his hands, and he
stood between J.T. and the stairs to go up to the
reception area.

"Hey, take it easy. You almost ran me down."

"Sorry," he muttered, anxious to get up the stairs
and find Vonya. "I wasn't looking."

"What's wrong?"

J.T. exhaled harshly. "What are you talking
about? You're married, and from what I can tell, to
a pretty wonderful woman."

"Oh, I'm perfect—wet, but perfect. I was talking
about you. You look as if you've lost your best
friend." That brought a smile to Jack's face. "I'm
just married, not dead," he said, gripping J.T. by
one shoulder. "Cheer up."

"I intend to," J.T. said as a white-coated waiter
came within arm's length with a tray of champagne
flutes. Jack ignored the drinks, but J.T. took one and
drank it quickly.

That drew a low whistle from Jack. "Is it that
bad?"

J.T. wondered what degree of "bad" would
match the rush of feelings he was having because
of the sudden appearance of Candice in his life
again. "No, it's nothing."

"I'd hate to see *something*," Jack muttered.

J.T. motioned vaguely behind him to the couple
on the sand. "How in the hell did that happen? You

said I wouldn't have to put up with the Montgomerys.''

Jack looked past J.T., then said, "I saw you talking, but I didn't know she'd gotten to you like that. Not after you assured me that the past was the past.''

"I'm just asking a question, and no, she didn't 'get to me,'" he said, wondering how he could lie so easily.

"Sandi just told me that Karl got her at the airport, that he even had the dress done so it fit her. Sandi was beside herself when Whitney and Dylan got stranded by the hurricane, and Karl stepped in to take care of it. I didn't know what that meant, until I saw Candice coming down the stairs.''

He finished his second glass and looked around for the waiter again. "Damn it, where did the waiter go?''

"I said cheer up, not get drunk." He glanced at Candice and Mark again. "It's not the end of the world.''

"It sure as hell isn't," J.T. said when he caught the waiter's eye and the man started across the sand to where he stood. He took another full glass, then he turned and looked at Jack. "And I'm not getting drunk. No self-respecting Texan would get drunk on champagne.''

Jack was staring at him hard, but with no trace of a smile. "I'll be damned," he whispered.

"Why are you looking at me as if I suddenly had two heads?''

Jack tugged the towel off his shoulders and scrubbed it across his face, then over the top of his head, spiking his hair slightly. "I was right, wasn't I?''

"About what?"

"You and Candice."

"Oh, no, don't start that again or I'm walking. No toasts, no rice. Nothing. That's way over, and she's got her overgrown yuppie that good old dad would have thoroughly approved of." He drank most of his new drink. "More power to her."

"Jack." Sandi was there, as wet as her groom, with a towel around her shoulders and her dress limp. She hugged Jack's arm and smiled at J.T. "Hey, you two. You look way too serious. What's going on?"

"Just talking," J.T. said.

"J.T., Jack doesn't need any 'guy advice,' thank you very much."

"So, he's got you fooled," J.T. said, mustering a smile.

"No, I know it for a fact," Sandi said, a bit of color touching her cheeks. Then she took a deep breath. "So, can I have my husband back? Are you finished with him?"

"Take the guy and good luck to you." J.T. raised the champagne glass. "To the two of you."

"Thanks, J.T.," Jack said. "And thanks for being here. I just wish Dylan could have made it, too."

"You got one Montgomery in the wedding. For most people, that would be more than enough."

Sandi frowned at J.T. "Have you and Dylan had a disagreement?"

"No, nothing like that," he said. "I don't have a problem with Dylan, except the fact that he's a Montgomery, and he couldn't help that." He narrowed his eyes, very aware of Candice somewhere behind him with Mark's ring on her finger and

Mark's arms around her. God, the idea nauseated him.

"I'm sorry I asked," she said with a weak smile.

Patrick came running over to them, heading right for J.T. The boy grinned at Jack and Sandi, then tugged on J.T.'s sleeve to get him to bend down. When he did, he whispered in his ear, "Uncle J.T., do you know about the surprise?"

"What surprise?" he asked, thinking that seeing Candice was more than enough of a surprise for him.

Patrick looked at Jack and Sandi, who were sidetracked talking to Karl Delaney for a moment, then he tugged J.T. a bit farther from them before whispering, "Fireworks. Mr. Delaney told me that they're going to shoot off fireworks and it's a surprise, 'cuz Dad and Sandi don't know nothing about it. Isn't that cool?"

J.T. smiled at his godson. "Way cool," he whispered.

"Hey, you two, we need to get pictures taken as soon as we get changed," Sandi said.

Patrick moved back and grimaced at J.T. "Pictures. Ugh."

J.T. tweaked his nose. "You'll look very cool in them."

Patrick turned and asked Sandi, "Do we have to put our shoes back on?"

"Just for the pictures, honey. Then you can take them off again."

"Okay." Patrick looked at J.T. "You coming up soon? Some real tall lady told me if I saw you, to tell you to go up there right away."

"I'm coming," J.T. said.

Sandi and Jack went first, but when Patrick started

to follow them with J.T. at his side, Karl stopped him. "Patrick," he said, coming up to the small boy and ruffling his hair slightly. "Do not tell too many people about the secret or it will not be a secret any longer."

"I just told Uncle J.T.," the boy said with a serious face. "That was all right, wasn't it, sir?"

"Surely. But no one else until it is time, okay?"

"Okay," Patrick said, then grimaced. "Oh, I sort of told someone else. I'm sorry."

"Who would that be?"

"This lady that knows Uncle J.T. She's real tall and got silver nails and said she loves secrets."

J.T. hadn't even noticed Vonya's nail polish, but he didn't doubt the silver part.

"Okay, but no one else. It must be a surprise," Karl said with mock seriousness. "Promise?"

"Cross my heart," Patrick said seriously as he crossed his heart. "Promise."

"Good boy," Karl said, then checked his watch. "It will only be for one hour, then the secret will be out."

"Oh, that long? I don't think I can wait."

"Waiting is part of the fun," Karl said, smoothing his mustache with his forefinger. "Why don't you run on up there and figure out where you will sit for the best view?"

"Yeah, sure," the boy said. "Uncle J.T., let's go and we can get a real good place."

He wanted nothing more than to go up to the high terrace with the boy, to leave Candice and Mark somewhere behind him on the beach. But Karl stopped him. "Can I talk to you for a moment?"

J.T. motioned Patrick to go on, then turned to

Karl. He had no idea what the man wanted to say
to him, but he knew what he wanted to ask him.
''Jack tells me that you were the one who lined up
Candice to take Whitney's place?''

''Oh, yes. When my niece called to say she could
not make it, I felt responsible to fix things for Sandi
and Jack. And since Candice is a very special friend
of both Whitney and Sandi, I thought it appropriate
that she fill in for Whitney.'' He smiled. ''Besides,
she looks stunning in that dress. Just a few nips and
tucks and it fit her perfectly.'' Karl was looking past
J.T., and he smiled. ''She is lovely, and will un-
doubtedly be a lovely bride.''

J.T. didn't turn. He didn't have to know who Karl
was talking about. Not when the man's words
brought back an image of a bride eight years ago.

Chapter Three

The chapel by the hotel had been determinedly ro-
mantic, with cupids everywhere, pink and red pre-
dominating the color scheme and artificial flowers
lining a short aisle that ended at a white podium
draped with roses.

The bride had been in jeans, with a cropped pink
sweater and her blond hair caught in a high pony-
tail. The bride had carried daisies he'd bought by
the door, and he hadn't been able to tell if she wore
any makeup or not. But she'd been achingly lovely.
Her blue eyes shadowed by those improbably long
lashes, her pale pink lips softly parted as Candice
had looked up at him....

He cleared his throat, wishing he knew a way to
kill whatever was dredging up the past so effectively. "Brides are all supposed to be lovely," he
said.

Karl glanced back at him, his eyes narrowed under his gray eyebrows. The man's bearing was ram-
rod straight in his dark jacket, beautifully cut on his
tall frame. "Yes, that seems to be a tradition," he
murmured. "So many of the ones I have watched
grow up are married."

J.T. could remember Karl quite clearly from the past, a presence, yet never in the middle of things. On the fringes. Sort of the way he'd been. The man had been there, watching. "You said you wanted to talk to me about something?" he asked, not wanting to talk about brides anymore.

"Did I?" Karl looked genuinely puzzled for a moment, then he smiled with a touch of embarrassment. "Oh, I am sorry. Excuse me. I must be getting old."

The man was probably in his late fifties or early sixties, not exactly ancient. "Everyone forgets now and then," J.T. said automatically.

That brought a chuckle from Karl. "Thank you for trying to make me feel better." Then his eyes widened. "Oh, I remember." He reached in his pocket and took out a folded piece of paper. "You dropped this earlier, and I was returning it," he said, holding it out to J.T.

He took it, vaguely remembering something about a piece of paper at some point this evening. This didn't look familiar, ivory and neatly folded into a two-by-two square.

He glanced back at Karl, those blue eyes touched by a look that J.T. realized he remembered from the past. The man had a way of looking at you as if he knew something no one else did, but J.T. had never been able to figure out just what that something was. He still couldn't. "I dropped this?"

"Yes, earlier."

He opened the paper, and in the dim light, he could barely make out a couple of lines written in precise script. *"When there is love, you are married forever."*

"This isn't mine," J.T. said, and held the note out to the other man.

"It is not mine." Karl shrugged, but he didn't take the paper back. "Keep it. Things usually end up where they belong."

J.T. blinked at him. "What?"

"Do what you will with it," Karl said.

He'd throw the note away, he thought, but just nodded and pushed it into his jacket pocket. Then he remembered. The paper, feeling it in his pocket during the ceremony. He could have slipped it out without even realizing, he'd been so distracted by Candice. Maybe the man who had worn this tux before had left it there.

He looked around, ready to go up the stairs. "If you'll excuse me?" he said.

Karl absentmindedly reached out and smoothed the material on the front of J.T.'s jacket. "Sir, you wear my work well."

"You sound surprised."

"One is always surprised when a rough diamond becomes polished and brilliant."

J.T. laughed at that. "A rough diamond?"

"I am sorry if I offended you," Karl said quickly. "I forget my place from time to time."

His place? The man had been the tailor to kings and world leaders. Yet he spoke of his "place." That sat badly with J.T., maybe because he'd been made to feel his place a time or two. At the hands of Candice's father, John Montgomery, as a matter of fact. "Sir, you didn't offend me, believe me. I'm a Texas cowboy who happens to be good at business. A rough diamond, as you say. No apologies."

"Yes, no apologies," Karl echoed.

Laughter cut into their conversation, soft female laughter that seemed to shimmer in the night. Candice. J.T. stared hard at Karl. "This is one rough diamond who is getting hungry."

"Ah, yes, food. They say they have a veritable feast up there."

J.T. could feel Candice getting closer, then he heard her voice in a soft murmur, the words indistinguishable but the tone intimate. Then they were there, Candice and Mark, hand in hand, stopping to say hello to Karl. He wasn't at all sure what they were talking about, and he knew he should walk away, but he didn't. He watched Candice, her eyes shadowed by the evening, her lips softly curved in a gentle smile. She simply glanced in his direction, and the sudden lurch in the region of his stomach was very real.

Damn it, everything blurred for him, and it took him a minute to realize that Karl was talking to him.

"Excuse me?" he said.

"I was just saying that tonight seems to be very special." He smiled at J.T. "A night for surprises."

J.T. didn't miss the way Candice's expression tightened or the way her hands moved to grip Mark's arm, her fingers pressed into the fine material of his jacket. "Are there more surprises?" she asked in that soft voice that held more velvet than the night and as much heat as a fire.

"Oh, yes, more surprises," Karl said.

J.T. waved away a hovering waiter. The champagne he'd drunk wasn't helping. Not when all he had to do was look at Mark. With Candice on his arm, he looked like a man who had just been handed the world. He'd been in that world once, for a single heartbeat, a very long time ago. He could almost hate Mark for being there now.

Patrick was next to him again, jumping up and down. "Uncle J.T., you said you'd be right up. Come on. I told that lady that I'd get you, and Sandi says they need to take pictures." He'd taken off his tuxedo jacket and the hem of his shirt was hanging out below his vest. "Sandi says we have to stay dressed until then." He grabbed J.T.'s hand. "Come on. Please."

He glanced at Karl, then past him to Candice and Mark. "Sorry, I'm going to have to get up there."

Candice turned away from him, held on to Mark as she said, "Let's go, Mark."

He watched them walk away together, arm in arm, going up the stairs, into the softness of the night, and he jumped when Karl touched his shoulder, urging him forward. "Come. The boy cannot wait."

J.T. fell in step with Karl, starting up the stairs behind Candice and Mark. "Do you know Mr. Forester?" he asked out of the blue.

J.T. refused to look up at the couple. "Just by reputation. But her family must be ecstatic that she's with someone like him."

"I think her family is very pleased with recent developments."

"That figures."

Karl sighed. "Seeing lovers together could almost make one jealous, couldn't it?"

J.T. stopped on the top step and let Candice and Mark get farther ahead of them on the way to the terrace area where the wedding guests were gathering. Jealous? He almost laughed at that. Jealous of a Mr. Yuppie? But no laughter came when he saw Mark bend to brush a kiss against Candice's cheek.

His stomach knotted and misery touched a part of his soul that he didn't even know still existed. My God, was he jealous? That thought hit him so hard he couldn't breathe for a moment. How could he be jealous of something he'd never really had? He turned abruptly from that sense of intimacy that Candice and Mark radiated.

You had to have something in order to be jealous of someone else having it. That only made sense. Candice was still very attractive. Okay, she was sexy. He could admit that. And it was one thing to still be turned on by whatever it was in the woman that had first attracted him. To remember the passion and the heat that had been there between them.

He spotted the bar set up on the terrace and made his way over to it. Jealous of Candice and some overgrown yuppie, who probably had the stamp of "Daddy Approved" on parts of his body? But images of a man touching and loving Candice were far too vivid, and he was startled when someone grabbed his arm.

"Darling, there you are." Vonya was there, incredibly beautiful at that moment. She'd never been possessive, never had a problem with him doing his own thing when they went out together. There had never been demands for attention, and he'd appreciated that. It made things very simple and uncomplicated, but right then she seemed almost to be pouting. "I was wondering when you'd remember I was here."

"Sorry," he said, then ordered a straight whiskey. "I ran into some people."

"This was such a good idea you had. I wasn't too sure, a small town and all of that," she said, and he noticed she had a drink in her free hand. Obviously, she'd had a bit to drink. "But it's very, very nice. I just wish we didn't have to leave so soon. But I have to be in Saint Tropez so soon." She took a drink. "Would you come with me?"

Candice and Mark were just down the bar talking to Sandi and Jack, the four of them laughing together. Candice brushed a hand lightly over her hair, catching at a slight curl by her temple and smoothing it. He really liked her hair longer, the silkiness lying soft against his skin.

He shook his head and reached for his whiskey before he glanced at Vonya. "What'd you say, darlin'?"

"Saint Tropez, it's wonderful this time of year. Why don't you come with me and we can have some fun?"

He turned his back on the four down the bar, and concentrated on Vonya. "Saint Tropez? No, I have to head back to London, but when I'm done there, I'm going to the ranch." He took a sip of the whiskey and let its fire fill him, when he realized he didn't want to go back to the ranch alone. "How about meeting me at the ranch in a few days?"

That made her laugh. "I can't take off for Texas and horses and cows. I have to be in Manila after Saint Tropez." She got closer and smiled seductively at him. "But we have now."

"I can't just pick up and go to the ranch with you," Candice had said. *"What about my family? I have to give them time to get used to all of this."* She'd moved closer to him. *"But we have now."*

He'd wanted nothing more than to take Candice to the ranch, to have the long, hot Texas nights with her, and he'd fully expected her to go with him when they left Nevada. He'd been wrong, very wrong. He took another drink of the whiskey, and focused on Vonya. "Yeah, that's about all we have, isn't it?" he murmured.

She cocked her head to one side. "Exactly, so let's make the most of it." She took the empty glass out of his hand to put it on the bar, then she had him by the hand, tugging at him. "Okay, I have to leave soon and so do you, so why not make the most of this moment? Listen to that music coming from the ballroom. Let's dance."

He looked at her and realized how right she was. All he had was now. He curled his fingers with hers and nodded, "Darlin', you're on. Let's dance, and enjoy ourselves, then you go to Saint Tropez, and I'll ride off into the sunset."

She laughed at that as they started across to the open doors of the ballroom. "You've got a deal, cowboy," she said as they stepped through the doors and she turned to slip into his arms.

J.T. pulled her to him, felt her lean into him, and they started to move to a slow song. Automatically he kept time, mingling with the other dancers, but something wasn't working.

For a moment he thought he caught the scent that clung to Candice. A light, soft fragrance that had been unique to her. Odd that he'd remember a smell. He closed his eyes, inhaling the rich spicy scent that Vonya used, letting it wipe out all else.

He was startled when Vonya shifted, looping both of her arms around his neck and pressing her hips against his. She was looking at him, her expression quizzical. "Hey, cowboy, where are you?"

They kept moving together. "Right here, darlin'."

She shook her head. "Oh, honey, you're not even in the same room with me." She didn't look angry, just puzzled. "What's going on with you? You've been acting strange since the wedding ceremony."

He wasn't going to go into this with her. Not here, not now. "I'm fine," he said.

"You could have fooled me. I'm not used to dancing with a man and having him hold me like he was my father."

That made him grin. "Any man dancing with you doesn't have paternal thoughts. I've just got things on my mind."

"If it's work, forget it. I have."

"It's not work."

"Oh, I get it. Of course. The wedding made you uneasy, didn't it?" She smiled at him. "Relax, cowboy, I don't have any ideas along that line. Marriage isn't even in my vocabulary, not any more than it's in yours. I think we'll both end up old and unmarried and having fun."

Why did that scenario sound so pathetic to him? He pulled her back to him, letting her rest her head on his shoulder. Then, over her head, he saw Candice and Mark approaching the dance floor. He watched while Candice went into Mark's arms and the two started to dance. She smiled up at him, then turned her head to rest it on his shoulder. And right then, J.T. saw a flash of complete sadness on her face.

It was there, then gone, but it was the same look

he'd seen on her mother's face years ago. He wasn't sure if he'd imagined it, but he wasn't imagining the way it wrenched him on some level to think that she wasn't happy. That was crazy. She had her fiancé, her money, her world as a Montgomery, but maybe happiness was eluding her the same way it seemed to have eluded her mother.

From nowhere came the thought that all he'd ever wanted for her was her happiness. A noble thought, for sure, but a very true one. He'd cared, and on some level, he felt a sense of protectiveness about her. Even when they'd parted, he hadn't wanted her hurt.

Vonya said something he didn't catch, then did an intricate dance step before twirling out, then back into his arms. His hands spanned her waist as he looked into her face. For now she was exactly what he needed, a refuge from every complication that Candice brought with her. But before he left, he wanted to know one thing...if he'd imagined the sadness or if it was very real.

CANDICE WENT into Mark's arms as they got to the dance floor. But right then, the slow music stopped and a fast piece started. She looked up at Mark, ready to tell him she'd pass, that she didn't feel all that steady right now, but he was pulling her to him before she could say a thing.

She stumbled, trying to get in step with him, and knew where the unsteadiness in her legs had come from. J.T. Damn it, that was one thing she remembered all too well from the past. Just looking at J.T. had made her legs weak. A hormonal response, obviously, but still there.

Now she was in Mark's arms, being supported as he laughed about her misstep. "Relax, enjoy," he whispered against her hair.

She turned to lay her head against the hollow of his shoulder, but she felt oddly alone, even though Mark was holding her. A sad loneliness came over her, something she'd never felt before. It was ridiculous. She was surrounded by people dancing. She was being held by the man she was going to marry in only a few months, but something was wrong. She just didn't know what it was.

She missed her step again and looked at Mark. "This isn't my kind of music," she said, moving away from him to head for the doors and out where she could breathe easier.

A burst of laughter caught her attention over the music, and she automatically glanced back at the dance floor just as Vonya was twirling toward J.T. The woman threw her head back, sending her mane of dark hair whirling, then she was in J.T.'s arms again.

Candice felt her legs weaken, and she reached for Mark's arm. Damn it, the man still had it. He had the ability to get to her on a physical level. That had never changed, and that was scary. "I need some air," she said quickly.

He slipped his arm around her and walked with her onto the terrace. But before she could take a deep breath, she was surprised to see her mother there in front of her.

Grace Montgomery looked tiny and delicate in a soft lavender dress that she wore as smartly as she did everything, even casual clothes. The sight of her was very welcome, and if she'd been given to bursts of emotion, Candice knew that she would have hugged her mother right then. But she settled for a smile and said, "Mother, I'm so glad you could make it. I thought you were going to…"

Her smile faltered and her voice trailed off as she realized that Grace wasn't listening to her, but staring at her dress, her pale eyes widening as her mouth formed a small *O*. Thank goodness Grace wasn't given to outbursts either, or Candice knew her mother would have been screaming. Instead, ever the lady, Grace came a step closer, her tiny hand reaching out to barely touch the scalloped hem of the skimpy top.

"My goodness," she whispered, but before she could say anything else, Karl was there, his gruff laughter filling the night air. The man obviously knew what Grace was thinking and probably knew how uncomfortable Candice was. That would explain a slight wink in her direction before he spoke.

"It is quite a remarkable creation, this dress," he said. "The rich colors of the setting sun, all combined to make Candice look exceptionally lovely tonight." He leaned toward Grace, his voice lowering, and his smile filling the blue of his eyes. "If it were acceptable to say it, one could say that the child is lovelier than the bride herself."

That brought faint color to her mother, brushing her delicate cheekbones as she drew her hand back and looked up at Karl. "No, that would not be acceptable," she murmured, her voice tight and, obviously, meant to be a reprimand for the man.

But he didn't take it that way. His smile was still intact as he got in his own slight jab at her mother's pomposity. "And one would not want to do anything that was not acceptable, would one?"

That deepened her blush, and Candice could see her mother stiffen at his words. Her look was cool when she turned it on Karl. "No, not at all," Grace said, dropping a wall between herself and the rest of them.

A disturbing observation, but something that Candice realized her mother had done all of her life. When she'd spoken with her father, that look had been there, that hiding behind a facade of rightness and manners, it was always there. Candice glanced at Karl. Even with Karl, who was just a friend.

"Pictures and shoes." Steffi was there, glancing down at Candice's gold pumps. "Good, you're all set. They want pictures to remember this by, so let's give them pictures." She motioned to the far side of the terrace to a smaller half circle that flared out over the bluffs for a spectacular view of the ocean.

She looked at Mark, then Grace and Karl. "She's mine for now," she said with a laugh, and looped her arm in Candice's. "Let's go."

Candice went gladly, hating the tension that she was feeling tonight, even with her mother. They were out of earshot of the people they'd left behind, when Steffi leaned closer to Candice and said, "So, what's wrong? Trouble with Mark?"

"No, of course not," she said.

"Well, you looked pretty upset when I rescued you."

She had to do a better job of controlling herself. "My mother's a bit upset over this dress," she said, a truth at least.

"Oh, I just bet she is," Steffi said as they approached the gathering for the pictures.

Candice stopped when she saw J.T. standing by Jack off to one side. Jack had changed into a plain dark suit, elegantly cut and not out of line with the tuxedo J.T. was wearing. They were talking. Then, as if in unison, they turned in her direction. The unsteadiness in her legs was back, and she was thankful that Steffi still had her by the arm.

"Hey, you'd think you were the nervous bride," Steffi said.

"I just hate having pictures taken," she muttered, looking away from the two men. "I always look as if I'm mad."

"I don't buy that. I bet even your driver's-license picture turned out perfect."

"Darlin', even your driver's-license picture is beautiful," J.T. had teased when she'd had to show it to the justice of the peace. *"I think I'll have it framed, and put it next to the wedding pictures."*

There had been a single Polaroid of the wedding, J.T. and her in front of the fake flowers. She had no idea where the picture had ended up. She couldn't even remember who'd had it last. It had probably been thrown away by the maid at the hotel.

"Candice, please, it's not that bad. All you have to do is stand very still and smile when they tell you to."

She tried to smile at Steffi, but knew her expression had to be a bit tight. It was hard enough to make her lips lift with any semblance of humor. "It's just a thing I have about being photographed. Some people are photogenic, and some aren't."

"Yes, like that woman J.T. brought with him. The

cheekbones on her. Wow... I'd give ten years of my life to have cheekbones like that.'' She laughed as they approached the photographer. ''And to weigh what she does. Did you see that dress? It's probably a size two.''

Candice tried to breathe, to ground herself, and it didn't help when she saw the object of their conversation standing talking with the photographer. Vonya turned when the two of them approached. ''You have the best photographer. He can do wonders.''

''As if she needs that,'' Steffi muttered just for Candice to hear, then she spoke up, ''Okay, if we're all here, let's get this over with.''

Sandi was there, wearing a lovely white gown, simple in cut, floor-length, with a delicate lace panel in front. Not a wedding dress, but close enough. Certainly not jeans and a sweater. Candice let go of Steffi and went to her spot on the opposite side of the wedding party from the men. She didn't look at J.T., even when she heard Vonya call out, ''Loosen up. You're all supposed to be having fun here.''

There was laughter at that, but Candice just stood there, willing it to be over. Then everything became a blur of posing and being posed. For those few moments, she could ignore Vonya who was behind the photographer now, peering at all of them, including J.T. Until Vonya took it into her head to get into the act. She said something to the photographer, then, suddenly, she was coming toward the group. ''Okay, let's have fun here. Mix and match!''

She was like a cyclone, arranging everyone close to the bride and groom, finally sitting the flower girl on the ground in front of everyone. She picked up the flower girl's rose-petal basket, stood to one side and called out, "Go," at the same time she tossed rose petals into the air.

The soft petals drifted in the air, falling around the wedding party while the photographer clicked away. Then Vonya was calling out for Jack and Sandi to kiss, then pick up Patrick and hold him between the two of them, and all the while, the petals drifted around them.

"Closer, closer," she called, obviously having fun, and Candice had to admit that if the pictures turned out at all, they'd be different and wonderful. Then Vonya was moving again, getting Jack and Sandi to go forward a bit, with Patrick in front with the flower girl. Candice had almost forgotten about J.T. in all the rush and laughter, at least until she realized that somehow they had ended up side by side.

J.T. glanced at her, an unreadable look on his face, then he was right next to her, his arm against hers, and Vonya was calling out to the photographer. "Take each of the bridal party in couples. Start here," she said, and Candice felt Vonya pushing her, forcing her to get closer to J.T.

Candice didn't know exactly how it happened, but the photographer was much closer, Jack and Sandi were out of the way, and she was posing with J.T. for a wedding picture.

Chapter Four

This couldn't be happening, Candice thought, but knew that it was really happening when J.T. deliberately put his arm around her waist. He'd only held her like this a half-dozen times in the short period they'd been together, yet in some odd way, it felt so right. His length along her body, his arm around her, that sense of being able to feel his heartbeat and absorb his body heat.

"Smile, darlin'," he murmured, and she shivered at the same time the flashbulb went off.

As soon as the light was gone, she pulled away from J.T. and he let her go. Without looking back, she crossed to where Steffi was standing talking to a waiter. "Steffi, have you seen Mark anywhere?"

She turned to Candice. "No, I haven't for a while." She frowned. "Are you all right? You look pale."

"Just a bit tired," she said, the lie coming easily when the only alternative was telling her about J.T. and his effect on her. "I just wondered where he'd gotten to."

"Can't stand to be away from him, can you? I know how it goes." She glanced past Candice. "I'm always looking for Greg.'' Then she smiled and Candice didn't have to turn to know that she'd spotted her new husband. ''I love to just see him.''

Right then she heard that laughter again, J.T., and she steeled herself against it. Hormones. That was it. Maybe some mixture with memories. That was all this reaction was to her.

''Darlin', you're crazy,'' she heard him say.

Vonya said something she couldn't make out as the music started up, then J.T. laughed again. It was a cruel trick that at the sound, despite everything, her legs almost buckled. Damned, stupid hormones, she thought and looked around for Mark. But he was still nowhere in sight. Then she saw her mother at one of the many small tables that had been set up on the rim of the terrace for the view.

She turned to go over to her, but stopped when she realized her mother wasn't alone. She was with Karl, sitting near the wall that rimmed the outer ridge of the terrace. The two of them were talking intently, no smiles, their heads inclined toward each other, and despite the fact they had a table separating them, they looked almost intimate.

She really was having trouble tonight, down to and including hallucinating, seeing things that weren't there. Her mother and a tailor? Hardly. That stopped her dead. How horrible. She was becoming her father. She could almost hear him saying, *''A Montgomery and a cowboy. I think not, Candice.''* That sickened her slightly, and she pressed a hand to her bare middle.

When a waiter offered her a flute of champagne, she gladly took it. Her father had been gone almost a year, and at first it had been wrenching for Candice, a hole in her life that had left her feeling oddly disconnected. But gradually, life had settled into a pattern, the same pattern it had taken when he was here. She worked as liaison at the head offices of the family-owned company, looking out for the estate, and she traveled and she saw Mark. She took a sip of champagne, wishing Mark was beside her, but she couldn't see him anywhere.

"The first dance as man and wife," someone announced, and she saw Jack and Sandi walk into the ballroom and go to the center of the floor as the others rimmed the outside. Candice stayed where she was, watching the two of them, the way they held each other and smiled at each other, then Jack kissed Sandi and her heart lurched. They loved each other. Simple. They really loved each other. Something others seemed to find so easy, she'd never even stumbled upon.

That thought shocked her. What was she thinking? She was in love with Mark. Of course she was. She liked him. He was a good man, and he was fun and bright and very handsome. Everything she could want in a man. That had to be love, didn't it? The kind that lasted forever? Love wasn't madness and heady craziness. Love wasn't forgetting everything just to have one touch. She drank the cool champagne, letting it spread to her middle. Love wasn't craziness, that desperate need for someone else.

This was all J.T.'s fault. All his fault. The man drove people crazy. He drove her crazy. After eight years of no contact, never even calling or coming back to Montgomery Beach to see Dylan, he still drove her crazy.

She finished her champagne, then turned to get

another…and almost dropped her glass when J.T. was right there. He was so close, she could see the way gold flared within his irises. She knew if she inhaled, the essence of the man would fill her, and that was the last thing she wanted.

And she certainly didn't want him to lean even closer and say for her ears only, ''Can we talk?''

Candice stared at J.T. He wanted to talk?

''We didn't do much talking before,'' he said in a low voice, and she didn't know if he did it on purpose, but his words brought a heat to her that was very unwelcome. There was no way to hide from memories of them not talking eight years ago.

''There's nothing to say,'' she said, hoping that would stop whatever was happening in its tracks. But she wasn't that lucky.

J.T. came even closer, and she hated the way she could see the fine lines etched at the corners of his mouth, and remember the way his lips had felt when they'd touched her skin. ''There's lots to say,'' he persisted and motioned toward the interior of the hotel. ''Can't we find a quiet place and finish this?''

Finish it? She looked into his hazel eyes. Would what he could do to her with one look ever be finished? ''Why aren't you roping cattle on that ranch of yours instead of coming here?''

''I came for Jack's wedding.''

''Why?''

''Why not?''

''You didn't come for Dylan's wedding.'' She'd been prepared for that, for seeing J.T. then, and had been overwhelmingly relieved when he'd backed out. But she wasn't prepared now. ''He's your friend, too.''

"Of course he is. A good friend." His expression tightened a little. "He's a Montgomery of honor. How unique."

"If you're going to bash my family, I'm not—" She turned to get away from him, but his touch on her arm stopped her dead. She should have jerked away, pulled back and broken the contact, but she couldn't move.

"I'm sorry," he said in a rough, low whisper. Then thankfully his touch was gone from her arm.

The last time she'd heard him say he was sorry was when he was apologizing for marrying her. "J.T., there's nothing left to talk about. You've got your life, and I've got mine. Whatever happened, happened so long ago and was so short, it isn't even a consideration now."

He studied her intently while she fought the urge to rub at the spot on her arm he'd touched. "Maybe you're right," he said, but didn't leave it there. "Just tell me one thing."

"What?"

"Are you happy?"

That jarred her. "That's a ridiculous question."

"Not that ridiculous," he said, narrowing his eyes on her.

"Why would you even ask that?"

"You don't look happy."

Everything about the man was still the same, despite eight long years of time passing between them. He could say words that trapped her, then say words that made her wish she could remember what she was supposed to do. A part of her knew that the craziness he'd brought out in her back then was still somewhere deep inside her. He hadn't changed, and there was the very real prospect that she wasn't that far removed from the girl who had impulsively run off and married him, either.

She was older, but apparently not much wiser. She stared at J.T., at the tan that wasn't quite as deep as it had been, the hair touched by a suggestion of gray at the temples, fine lines at his eyes and mouth. But there was still a lean sensuality about him, devastating in jeans and cowboy boots, but just as disturbing in Karl's well-tailored tuxedo.

"You don't even know me, J.T., you never did, so how can you judge whether I'm happy or not?"

He was still staring at her, and it was unnerving her. "Oh, I know you," he whispered. "And I can see it in your eyes."

Without warning, he reached out and his finger feathered a touch on her cheek, then it was gone before she could begin to absorb any reaction to the contact.

"Bullsh—" She cut off her response, but not before she saw a smile come to his face—a flashing, endearing expression that lit up his hazel eyes and drew painfully at something buried so deeply inside her, she couldn't begin to define what it was.

"Were you going to say what I think you were going to say?" he said, an all-too-familiar teasing tone from the past filling his voice. "Whatever would Grace say about her little darling resorting to profanity?"

Why did he have to be so annoying and so endearing at the same time? "Why don't you ask her?" she muttered, motioning to her mother nearby, deep in conversation with Karl.

J.T. glanced over at the two people, then back at

Candice. "When did she get here?" Any humor was gone.

"A while ago."

"Grace Montgomery late for a wedding? Now, that's a first," he said, that edge in his voice.

"And none of your business," she said, hoping to cut off any further conversation. But it didn't work.

He studied her, then unexpectedly brushed the tip of his finger along her jawline. This time she did react. She jerked back, hiding a sudden trembling in her being and putting a bit of distance between them. "Don't do that," she said through clenched teeth.

"You know, Jack had to talk like hell for me to agree to come here for the wedding," he said as he drew his hand back and pushed it into the pocket of his tux jacket.

"You didn't want to come?"

"To this place? Hell, no. What does a common cowboy want in a place like this?"

"A *common* cowboy?" she echoed.

"Isn't that what your father used to call me? A great friend for Dylan, the money and the business and all, but when it came to anything beyond that, well, darlin', I was common, my money was common and I was unacceptable."

She was shaking and clasped her hands tightly in front of her. "Father never said that to you."

"But he did to you, didn't he?" His eyes narrowed, and she didn't miss the tightness at his mouth. "Candice, princess," he said in a fair imitation of her father's abrupt way of speaking. "James Taylor Watson is a nice fellow, a good friend to Dylan, a man of some means, but he's so…so…'' He waved a hand in a dismissive gesture that mimicked her father's actions perfectly. ''Common. Not one of us. So, be nice to him, but not too nice. He's definitely not nice enough for my little girl, the princess, the chosen one.''

Her stomach hurt, and words caught in her throat. That wasn't exactly what her father had told her all those years ago, but close enough to bring fire to her cheeks. ''Shut up,'' she hissed. ''Don't you talk about Father like that.''

''Still defending him, aren't you, him and his god-awful prejudice.'' He was so close to her now, she could feel him exhale, the heat brushing her bare skin, and she had no idea how he'd managed to compromise the distance she'd managed to build between them. ''God, I thought after…'' His words faded off, then he shook his head. ''So much for stupid ideas,'' he muttered.

When J.T. looked back at her, there was a flash of something in his eyes. But she knew she was reading the man wrong, probably the way she always had. That couldn't be pain she saw, no, it had to be anger. She was as wrong as she'd been before, thinking she saw love there eight years ago.

He moved his hand as if to brush her away from him. ''Go and find Mark what's-his-name, and do your father proud.''

She had a hard time even thinking about Mark, much less moving away to find him. ''Don't tell me what to do,'' she breathed, and knew if she was ever going to take another normal breath, it would only come when J.T. Watson was nowhere around.

"Don't look at me like that," he whispered harshly.

"L-like what?" she managed to say in a horribly unsteady voice.

He shook his head again, a sharp motion, and muttered, "Like you're afraid of me."

"I'm not," she said without much conviction.

Those hazel eyes were on her again for a long moment. "Damn it," he said softly. "I'm slow, but I finally get it."

"What?" she asked, because she didn't get it at all.

"You've never told Mark about us, have you?"

She swallowed hard at the question. The idea of saying anything to Mark about a twenty-four-hour marriage that was over before it began was so far from her thoughts that she had a hard time grasping the concept.

He answered his own question before she could think of what to say. "Of course you didn't. Just the same way you never told your mother or father, or even Dylan."

Why were his words hurting her so much? It wasn't the idea of anyone knowing about what they'd done that hurt, it was this man looking at her as if he actually hated her right then. She didn't want hate. "J.T., that's not fair, I never said—"

"No, you never did. Don't worry, darlin', it wasn't important then, and it sure as hell isn't important now. So, don't worry. I'm not going to say anything to anyone."

Was she supposed to thank him for saying that something that had almost torn her life apart wasn't important, that it never had been to him? She bit her lip hard, trying to figure out what to do or what to say, but she never had to make that decision. Not when J.T. turned and walked away without another word.

She was alone, and a surprisingly warm breeze off the ocean was making her tremble as badly as if it had come down from the Arctic. "Damn it," she muttered, hating the way her eyes burned, and hating the echoes from the past caused by a man who could hurt her with words.

"Hey, I've been looking all over for you."

Candice turned and Mark was there—sane, safe Mark. Before she even thought about it, she went into his arms, holding on to him for dear life.

J.T. CROSSED THE TERRACE, spotted Jack and Sandi and headed for them. He'd come, he'd worn his tux barefoot, he'd seen Jack married and it was time to find Vonya and go.

As he approached Jack, he glanced over his shoulder and felt real distaste when he saw Mark holding Candice in his arms. Even that was off kilter, mingling with something that was beginning to make him feel as if he were breaking apart.

He'd drunk the last of his drink, looked around for a waiter to get a refill, but instead found Vonya there, holding two flutes of champagne.

"You are so hard to track down," she said, offering him one of the flutes. "The guests are starting to settle out here for dinner under the stars, and since you are the best man, I believe you'll be at the head table for the toasts and everything."

J.T. had all but forgotten about any duties he had

as best man, so leaving right away was obviously, out of the question. "I never thought of that."

"Well, I did," she said. "And take this."

He put his empty glass down on a side table and took the champagne flute. "Thanks."

"Sure," she said, wrapping her arm around his and getting closer to him. "Now, the thing is, if you're at the head table, I have to sit somewhere, and since I don't know too many people here, I'm not sure where to sit."

"I can help you there," Karl said as he approached the two of them. He bowed slightly to Vonya. "I am Karl Delaney, and I have a table that is much too big for me. Would you do me the honor of being my dinner companion?"

"Oh, that's lovely. Yes, thank you." She looked at J.T. "Isn't that sweet?"

"Very," he said.

She looked back at Karl and slipped her hand in the crook of his arm. "Lead the way, Mr. Delaney," she said. "I heard that you have made clothes for so many famous people." She grinned at him. "I bet you know all the dirt on some pretty big names?"

"Part of my business is being very discreet, sort of like a psychiatrist or an attorney."

"Oh sure," she said, walking away with him. "But you can trust me."

J.T. watched them go. Karl was a match for her.

He glanced around the terrace and spotted Sandi and Jack being seated at the head table in the same area where they'd taken pictures earlier. Steffi was there, motioning toward him to come over to the table. He headed across the terrace, very aware that

Candice wasn't among the group, although there was an empty chair between Steffi's and Sandi's chairs.

He slipped into his chair and glanced at Jack beside him. He was busy kissing Sandi, a kiss that seemed to last forever. Then Jack sat back and saw J.T. "Marriage," he said, grinning ear to ear. "Nothing like it."

"I never would have pegged you for getting such a bad case of love sickness," he mumbled, putting his champagne glass on the table.

"If this is being sick, never invent a cure," he said with a grin. "Too bad you aren't infected."

"I've got my diversions."

"I said 'love sickness,' not 'lust sickness,' J.T."

"I've given up on anything that complicated," he said, fingering his champagne glass.

"Never say never. Never give up."

"And sometimes you have to learn to say that's it, and walk," he said, not even sure where those words came from until they were out...until he saw Candice and Mark coming out onto the terrace from the ballroom. If he hadn't walked away from Candice all those years ago, God knows where he'd be today. A lapdog for her dad? A bitter man tied to a woman who put her family above everything and everyone? Not a pretty picture.

"Sometimes you just have to refuse to give up," Jack said. "Thank God I didn't give up on Sandi. It's the smartest thing I ever did."

"You're smart, man, I've always known that," J.T. said.

A guest stopped in front of where Jack and Sandi

were seated, and soon Jack was drawn into a conversation.

J.T. sat back, unbuttoned his jacket and pushed his hand into the pocket. He felt the piece of paper, the one he'd forgotten about. He drew it out, opening it briefly. *"When there is love, you are married forever."*

It should have been in Jack's pocket, he thought as he refolded the paper. Then he looked up and Candice was there, taking the seat next to Steffi, and his hand clenched, crushing the paper still in it. Yes, it was for Jack. Not for him at all.

He watched Candice while she settled and accepted a flute of champagne before starting to talk to Steffi.

Forever? It hadn't even lasted twenty-four hours. Had he thought he'd been in love back then? He couldn't remember. There had been that burning need to be with her, to surround her and become part of her.

He shook his head. Was that love? Or was that what Jack had called "lust sickness?" He didn't have a clue. He only knew it had never happened again to him. Not even with Vonya. He'd never even wondered about that before. Great, another question to eat at him. Funny how they all centered around Candice.

He looked down at the piece of crumpled paper, then tossed it onto the table as the need for answers loomed very real. He was a man who liked to understand what was happening to him, who needed to, but right then he didn't have a clue. It was crazy. He should be thinking about Jack and Sandi, or the merger, or at least Vonya. But he was thinking about

Candice, about what there had been, and how he
could make sense out of it.

CANDICE NEVER LOOKED OVER at J.T., even though
they were both at the head table. Instead, she talked
to Sandi's sister, drank champagne, nibbled on her
food, drank champagne, watched her mother talking
to Mark, watched Vonya actually flirting with Karl
of all people, drank champagne, and ignored J.T. By
the time J.T. stood and asked for everyone's attention, he was a mere blur to her, a fantasy image that
she didn't have to focus on or worry about.

"Guests, friends, family, it's my honor to toast
Jack and Sandi, to wish them the best of everything
in their life together, and—" He turned to Patrick,
who had found his way onto Sandi's lap. "To Patrick, who apparently had a bit of a hand in this
whole thing." Candice smiled as the others chuckled
and then applauded as Patrick scooted off Sandi's
lap, stood, looked around and bowed from the waist.

It was easier to relax now. Nothing really mattered. Nothing. She narrowed her eyes on J.T., blur-
ring his image even more, making it easier to think
of the past. J.T. riding up the winding driveway of
the Montgomery house with Dylan, there for the se-
mester break. J.T., lean and with an edge that Candice had never seen before. J.T. in tight jeans, boots
and with his ever-present Stetson, choosing to come
to Montgomery Beach for a visit instead of heading
back to his family ranch outside of Dallas.

Three times he'd come to the house, three times
he'd smiled at her, teased her, talked with her about
everything from sports to the meaning of life. She
fingered her champagne glass. They'd never run out

of things to talk about, J. T. Watson and Dylan's kid sister. Until that final summer, just after graduation, when he'd come for the last time and the talking was over.

He'd been different and so had she. The looks they'd exchanged had been almost uneasy, both aware that things had shifted. She'd gone from a teenage kid sister who never stopped talking, to a nineteen-year-old woman who was as tongue-tied as the teenager should have been. J.T. had still worn those jeans that clung like a second skin, still worn the boots and had suntanned skin, but he was older, ready to take over his father's businesses, to enter into a world of money and power.

Maybe she'd had a crush on him all along, she couldn't really remember now. But she clearly remembered that summer, the way one look from those hazel eyes had stirred a fire in her that she'd never known before. Until his touch stirred her and made her yearn for more. Until she knew that, no matter what, she wanted to be with him.

She was startled out of the past when there was a sudden, brilliant flash of color exploding in the western night sky. Sparkles snaked into the sky again, and more explosions followed, bathing the world in a luminous glow.

Candice was vaguely aware of the others oohing and aahing as each explosion pushed back the night with the beauty of sudden, vivid colors that came out of the shadows to dominate the world. The way J.T. had come out of nowhere to dominate her world, to make his own explosions, pushing back her night. She trembled at a particularly brilliant purple shower in the heavens. Why had she thought that? That J.T. had pushed back her night?

She looked at where he still stood by Jack, both men watching the impressive display, the colors flowing over them. Then darkness until the fireworks exploded again. Darkness. Nothing. The way it had felt when J.T. had walked away. The color had gone, along with the brilliance in her life.

Chapter Five

Candice bit her lip hard. Damn it, she'd been drinking too much. She had a good life and a wonderful future ahead of her with Mark. She looked around quickly and spotted Mark still sitting with her mother, but he had his back to the fireworks display while he talked on his cell phone.

She lifted her hand, hoping to catch his attention, needing him near her right then, but he kept talking intently, oblivious to the celebration around him. For an instant, he was her father, absorbed in business, closing out the rest of the world, then he was Mark again. His eyes caught hers and she motioned him to come over to her. He smiled, but held up his hand, extended two fingers to ask for a bit of time to finish his business.

She wished she had it in her to get up and run across the room to him and throw herself into his arms, but she didn't move. Instead, she tried to smile, ended up nodding, and the next instant he was turning away from her to keep talking.

A sense of aloneness washed over her, akin to the feeling she'd had on the dance floor. It only increased when she saw Jack reach for Sandi, kissing her with real passion as the fireworks died out. She had the oddest sensation of the world shimmering around her, floating strangely, still clinging to the colors of the fireworks. Swallowing hard, she took a breath and knew she needed fresh air. A foolish need, since she was outside on the terrace. Maybe it was space? She wasn't sure, but she wouldn't find what she needed here.

Quietly, while the orchestra started up again and couples made their way to the dance floor, she slipped out of her seat and, instead of heading into the hotel, she started across the worn cobbles to the stairs down to the beach. She'd gone down the same stairs what seemed an eternity ago for the wedding on the beach. An eternity since J. T. Watson had burst back into her life.

She reached for the railing at the same moment she knew she wasn't walking alone. Someone was right behind her and that someone was saying her name. "Candice?"

J.T. She closed her eyes for a fleeting moment, then without turning, she asked, "What?"

"I thought we could talk."

She thought he was joking. There was no way she wanted to talk to him anymore. She shook her head. "Why?"

"It's been a long time since we talked, and I thought there were a few things that needed saying."

"No."

That brought a humorless laugh. "No? That's it?"

"Leave me alone, J.T.," she said and, gripping

the railing tightly, started down the stairs on unsteady legs.

J.T. couldn't do that, and he knew it right then.
He couldn't leave her alone any more than the tide
could stop coming in and going out. He went down
the stairs after her. "What's going on here?" he
asked, but she didn't stop or turn when she spoke
back to him through the night.

"I'm going for a walk. Alone."

"In those shoes?" he asked as she reached the
sand and her gold heels sank into the silty surface.

She stopped, gripped the railing with one hand
and slipped off her shoes. Without a word, she set
them by the bottom step, then started across the
sand. He could see the unsteadiness in her step, but
she kept going toward the water.

He ignored his own shoes and headed after her,
wondering when he'd started running after women.
He'd never done that in his life, even with Candice
the first time. He paced himself to stay a few feet
behind her, then she stopped and he stopped.

"J.T., go away," she said softly.

He stayed where he was, pushing his hands into
the pockets of his tux jacket. "I told you, I want to
talk."

"Why?"

He barely heard the single word on the night air.
"Because this doesn't make sense. Do you really
remember what happened, or how it happened? Or
even why?" He felt the crushed paper in his pocket
and couldn't even remember having put it back
there. "I don't, not really. I mean, sure I remember
some of it, but for the life of me, I don't remember
how we let it happen."

"You left."

"*You* left."

He saw her take a breath and her shoulders trembled. Damn it, the action touched his soul as she said, "Okay, you had to have it all your way. You wouldn't wait, or let me try and figure things out. It was either I went with you right then and turned my back on everything else, or you'd walk."

Had he been that cut-and-dried? Do it his way or forget it? He couldn't remember, only the moment when he'd known he'd lost. He was crushing the paper again as his hand curled into a fist. "Would you have gone against your father if he'd told you to get the hell away from me?"

Her sigh was deep and so sad. "That's not fair."

"Not fair?" He went closer, but stopped right behind her. "You're the one who said it was a mess and you couldn't do anything against your parents. Then you left."

"And you never came after me."

He froze, his heart lurching. "I didn't know you wanted me to."

She shrugged again, a sharper movement, a dismissive action. "I didn't expect you to."

"What if I had?"

"You wouldn't have. You'd made your thoughts very clear, and one thing I knew very well about you back then, you didn't bluff. You meant what you said." When she turned to him, he noticed that the low light and the duskiness blurred her features, hiding her eyes enough so the impact wasn't there. "You know, in that way, you were very much like my father."

"Don't even put us both in the same sentence," he muttered.

She was silent for a long moment, and the only sounds were the surge of the tide and the far-off sounds of the party. Then she said, "That sounds just like something he'd say about you."

Before he could think of what to say, she turned and was heading off toward an outcropping of rocks at a flare in the bluffs. He went after her again. He wasn't going to let her have the last word, especially that word. "He's still doing it, isn't he?"

She stepped up onto low rocks to stand above a shallow tide pool on the other side and look down at him. "He? He who?"

He stopped, looking up at her. "Your father."

"My father's dead," she said tightly.

"But he's still running the show, isn't he?"

"What are you talking about?"

"Is that why you're engaged to Mr. Approved By Daddy? Too bad you aren't in any rush to marry him. I'm sure it would make Daddy damn proud to get you married off to him."

He could see the way she bit her lip before she said, "When I marry Mark is none of your business."

He knew that, but he couldn't let it alone. "Sure, you're so nuts about him, you're thinking that a year down the road you might get married."

"I rushed it once. I won't make that mistake again."

Her words cut at him, and he found himself going closer. The sudden idea that he hated having no contact with her was there and solid. For eight years there had been nothing. Now, being here with her only made him wonder what it would have been like if they'd never married and if they'd just stayed friends. Friends who had talked about everything, and joked and watched old movies together.

But that wasn't what had happened. Now she was older, more reserved, and she had Mark. He studied her, the set of her mouth, the way she crossed her arms over her breasts and hugged herself. Something was wrong, and he had a thought that really bothered him. She was marrying Mark because of her father. To give her father what he would have wanted if he was alive today. Sacrificing herself, the way she'd sacrificed him eight years ago. That thought nauseated him.

He ran a hand roughly over his face before asking the one thing he had to know before he left. "Do you love him?"

"I'm marrying him," she said tightly.

"That's no answer."

Her eyes narrowed as if she couldn't stand looking at him and it knotted his stomach. "Mark's wonderful. He's stable and secure and caring."

"And he's been handpicked by your dad. Not bad qualifications, but hardly a reason to marry anyone, unless it's a merger for the sake of the company. From what I heard, Dylan was almost pulled into that sort of nightmare. Is that what's going on? He's in line to run the company, so you keep him happy by marrying him and producing the suitable heir?"

"You bastard," she muttered and, without thinking, her hand was moving, swinging toward his face. But she never made contact. As her hand swung out, the rocks under her feet shifted and, instead of going toward J.T. to slap him for what he'd said, she was flailing, then pitching backward, grabbing at thin air.

The next thing she knew, she was falling and twisting. Her last glimpse was a reflection of herself on the placid surface of the tide pool, then she plunged forward into the water. Coldness was everywhere. Water stung her eyes and filled her mouth and nose, then she felt heat and someone was grabbing her.

In a single action, she was being pulled back and out of the water, into cool air, but the hot contact was still there. She swiped at her stinging eyes, coughing out water, and realized that J.T. was steadying her in knee-deep water. She blinked, her eyes focusing, and he was there, his hands on her arms, so close that the only heat in the world came from him.

Then he laughed, the sound soft on the night air, and she could feel his body shaking with the humor. "Darlin', a bit of advice. If you're going to try to slap someone, make sure you're on solid ground," he said.

The man was standing in his tuxedo in a knee-deep tide pool, his clothes ruined and his shoes obviously beyond any help, and he was smiling and laughing about her trying to hit him.

She felt so confused, she could barely think of what to do, except to break the contact between them. She swiped at the stinging in her eyes again, then pulled back, trying to break that contact and the way the man's presence seemed to be surrounding her.

But the action stopped abruptly when she gasped as her foot pressed down onto something sharp. She jerked back, automatically reaching back to J.T., gripping his arm to keep from falling forward again. "Damn it," she choked out and couldn't understand why tears were mingling with the saltwater on her face.

It made no sense, not any more than it made sense that she wanted to just keep holding on to J.T. It had to be the champagne. The dizziness came from that—this fuzzy thinking, this stupidity.

"Are you okay?" he was asking.

She stared at her hand on his arm, then pulled back, forcing herself to put a distance between them and stand carefully, barely touching the bottom of the pool with her sore foot. "I...I stepped on something, but I'm fine," she said, making herself move away from him again.

Without looking at J.T., she walked gingerly through the knee-deep pool to the rock rim and up onto the sand. Careful not to put her full weight on her right foot, she knew J.T. was there, very close, but she never turned as she limped across the sand away from the water. At the bottom of the stairs, she stopped and reached for the support of a waist-high stone wall that framed the way up to the terrace. Her shoes were still there, but she knew there was no way she could put them on, much less walk up the stairs.

Her foot was throbbing and she kept it inches off the sand and any pressure on it. She sensed J.T.'s presence to her left before she actually heard him say anything. "Let me look at your foot," he said.

She didn't want his touch, but before she could tell him to leave her alone, he caught her off guard by spanning her waist with his hands and easily picking her up. The next thing she knew, she was sitting on the wall and he was standing in front of her, reaching for her foot.

His touch was achingly gentle as he examined her, then he was looking at her, almost at eye level. "No cut, just a nasty knot, probably only a bruise."

"So, you're a doctor now?" she asked, annoyed that she sounded slightly breathless.

That smile came as his hand lingered on her foot. "No, but I was a junior rodeo rider, and you have to have first aid for that."

She never knew that about him. So many things she didn't know about this man, and so many things she was better off not knowing. She drew her foot back and away from his touch. "Thanks," she murmured. "I need to get up to Sandi's room. They took our clothes there from the dressing room."

"No problem. I'll get you up there."

"I can do it by—"

"Yourself. I know." He stood back, his eyes narrowed. "Go ahead, let's see how you're going to do it."

"I don't need an audience," she muttered.

"No, but you might need a rescue party, and since I'm here…" He shrugged. "Why bother getting someone else to come on down to watch this. I'm here."

She hated him being there and watching, but arguing with him was useless. The man was stubborn. "Okay, fine, just get away. Stand over there." She flicked her hand in the direction of the water. "Far over there."

He took a step back, the most he was obviously going to do. "Can I point out something else?" he asked as she shifted on the rock wall, trying to turn around and slip off backward.

"Could I stop you?" she said as she leveraged herself down until she felt the sand under her uninjured foot.

"No."

She shifted, very carefully lowering her other foot to the sand, but even a fleeting contact made her wince. She gripped the wall and turned on one leg. "Then what is it?"

"I don't think that is how a Montgomery would want to make an entrance," he said, motioning to her soaking clothes, clinging hair and sore foot.

Damn it, she'd forgotten about the way she must look. The confusion of being around J.T. and trying to get away from him had robbed her of all common sense. But she had to get up to the hotel someway, and the stairs were the only way she knew of to do that. "I have to change, and my clothes are up in the hotel. I…" She looked up and down the length of the beach. "There has to be a way to do this."

"Will you let me make a suggestion?"

She looked back at J.T., thankfully keeping about a three-foot buffer of space between them intact. "All right, I'm open to suggestions."

"It seems to me that there's an elevator to the lower patio on the side of the hotel, down the beach. That might be an answer."

She narrowed her eyes to dull the image of the man in front of her. His hair was slightly wind-blown, a smile was a mere suggestion at his lips and his arms were crossed at his chest. His shoes were coated with sand, and sand strayed up on the wet area of his pant legs. He was right about the elevator. "I forgot about that."

He motioned along the beach. "A couple of hundred feet around the corner down there, and you're home free. You can sneak into the elevator, go up bypassing the lobby and no one ever needs to know." He reached toward her, but didn't touch her. Instead, he picked up her shoes, then straightened with the shoes hooked over his fingers. "And I can certainly keep a secret."

She looked away from him, not wanting to think about secrets and J.T. Using the wall for support, she tried to walk along the beach, but the first time she attempted to use her bad foot, she gasped and pulled it back from the contact.

"It hurts?" J.T. asked from somewhere to her right.

She nodded, biting her bottom lip.

"You can't walk?"

She exhaled and shook her head. "I guess I'll have to...to..."

"To what?"

She didn't know. She didn't have a clue. "I'll just wait a bit, and maybe—"

"You'll sprout wings so you can fly?"

She didn't want his humor, not when she felt anything but humorous right then. "I'll manage. You can go."

"Oh, I'm dismissed?"

She looked at him, then lashed out in frustration, "Yes, go, get out of here. I'll be okay."

He came closer and muttered, "This is ridiculous."

''Don't tell me what's ridiculous,'' she practically shouted. ''I'm a big girl. I can take care of myself.''

''You're still as stubborn as hell,'' he said, closer still.

''And you're an expert on stubborn women?''

''No, but I've dealt with a lot of stubborn cattle in my life,'' he said, leaning so close, she felt his breath on her face when he spoke. ''And I'm not sure that women are that much different.''

''We're like cattle?'' she said with a gasp.

''I didn't say that, I just said that you're both stubborn.''

Right then, voices drifted down the stairs, people obviously coming down onto the beach. Laughter and voices mingled, and Candice cringed. The last thing she wanted was to be found like this by anyone at the wedding. ''Oh, shoot,'' she muttered, trying to take more steps to get away from the stairs. But even trying to hop wasn't going to do it. She turned, J.T. was there. ''I can't believe that this is happening,'' she said.

''Neither can I,'' he said, then without warning, he was reaching out for her. Before she could think of what to do, he was lifting her high off the ground, but he wasn't cradling her in his arms. Something she expected, just as much as she dreaded it. Instead, he was tossing her over his shoulder like a bag of feed.

She kicked her feet and hit at his back. ''You let me down right now,'' she cried frantically.

''Calm down and be quiet, or they'll hear you,'' he said. ''I'd hate to have to hog-tie you.'' She didn't miss the touch of humor in his voice. He was enjoying this!

She wanted to scream and fight, but she knew he was right. If she did what she wanted to do, the people coming down would not only hear her, they'd also find her looking like a drowned rat and thrown over the shoulder of a macho cowboy.

She bit her lip hard, grabbed at his arm to keep from slipping, and as they rounded a curve in the bluff, blotting out any way someone could see them, she hissed, "J.T., stop, and stop right now!"

He kept going, and just as she was about to fight again, he stopped. He swung her down off his shoulder, onto tile that felt cold under her good foot. He held her by one arm, letting her get steady before letting go, and she looked around to find that he'd carried her all the way to the lower patio. They were right by the elevators.

He drew back, not touching her now; in fact, his hands were in the pockets of his jacket. But there was still that shadow of a smile at the corners of his mouth. "Your image is safe. No one's around to see you," he said softly. Then the smile was gone completely. "Not even your fiancé." He came a bit closer, robbing Candice of the air around her to breathe. "Okay, you can say it anytime now."

She pressed her hand hard against the closed door, fighting a slight light-headedness now that she could feel the air stir with J.T.'s movement. "Say what?"

"Thank you." He was so close, she was certain she could feel the heat of his breath when he exhaled before he said, "You weren't humiliated, because nobody saw you like this. You got to the elevator. A thank-you would be nice right about now and the proper thing to do, especially for a Montgomery."

She turned from J.T. to face the elevator door,

then saw the dull glow of the floor button off to the right side. As she reached to press the up button, she muttered, ''Thanks for everything.''

''That wasn't said with any sincerity.'' The teasing was there in his rough voice, running riot on her nerves and bringing back more memories.

''That's the best you're going to get,'' she said, staring hard at her blurred image in the polished metal door. The drops of moisture from the nearby ocean distorted her, making her wavy and insubstantial-looking, almost the way she felt at that moment. But she was a mess. That was very clear, as clear as the blurred image of J.T. behind her. ''Thank you.''

She bit her lip hard when he stayed silently behind her as the elevator car traveled down to the beach level. She just wanted him gone, to have him walk away. He'd done it perfectly eight years ago. Was that too much to ask for now, to let her breathe, to let her get her life back on level ground? She took a shaky breath. ''What do you want?''

She could hear him take a ragged breath, but he didn't say a thing. The silence between them was almost palpable, and it forced her to shift her hand and turn awkwardly. He was close enough for her to almost brush her arm against his open jacket as she turned, and he wasn't moving back an inch.

''What?'' she cried, nerves making her head lighter and her stomach knot.

''Nothing,'' he said simply, then pushed one hand into the pocket of his jacket and took something out. He held up a small piece of crumpled paper. ''I found this in my pocket earlier.''

She didn't understand. ''And?''

"It says, *'When there is love, you are married forever.'*"

The words only made her world more unstable, and it slipped even more when the door behind her opened and she felt a void at her back. Almost as big a void as she was starting to find inside herself with talk of love and marriage. Love hadn't even been in the picture for them. "I don't..." She had to swallow hard to control a sickness in her. No more words would come. Love? She couldn't even begin to think about that anymore.

"I read it and realized that no matter what anyone thinks, that if there isn't love, it's not a marriage. Maybe that's why the annulment was so easy for you to get."

There wasn't love. She knew that, but didn't understand why it hurt so much to hear him say it. "You mean, it was easy for *you* to get an annulment," she said, hearing the unsteadiness in her voice.

"Me? What are you talking about? I didn't get any annulment. In fact, I never even got a copy of the papers from you."

She closed her eyes tightly, light-headedness coming with a vengeance. "What?"

"You got the annulment," he stated.

She reached for the elevator doorjamb and tried to think. "No, you said..." She tried to remember what both of them had said on that last fateful day. "You...you said you'd get the annulment, that you'd end everything."

"No, I agreed to it and said, if you wanted it, to get it." He was so close, she heard each breath he took as he leaned toward her. "*You* got the annulment."

"N-no, I didn't," she stammered as a horrible thought exploded in her. "I never..." She had a brief thought that he was teasing again, but one look at his face told her this was no joke. "*You* never?"

"Never," he said, his eyes narrowing, then an odd smile touched his lips.

Candice wasn't smiling. She stared at J.T., horrified at the knowledge that if he hadn't taken care of the annulment, there hadn't been one. And if there wasn't an annulment, they had been married all this time. For the last eight years, while she'd gone on with her life alone, they'd been married.

"J.T.?" she said softly, but couldn't focus on him. He blurred and shimmered before her as the light-headedness took over for good this time. She grasped at the elevator door frame to ground herself, but it didn't do any good. She was floating, and her last thought before she fainted dead away was that life had just played its cruelest card. She was still married to J.T.

Chapter Six

J.T. saw the shock on Candice's face, then the way she paled. The next thing he knew, she was falling toward him and he was reaching out for her. In a blur he caught her, lifted her high into his arms, and realized that she had fainted.

"Candice?" he whispered as he looked around and spotted a stone bench near the elevators. He crossed to it, sat down with her on his lap and touched her face. She felt cool, but her breathing was even and natural. "Candice?"

The shadows of the night touched her exquisitely, exposing the hollows at her cheeks and defining the sweep of her throat. She was lovely, achingly lovely.

Her eyes fluttered slightly, then she shifted in his arms, turning toward him in his hold, and pressed her face into his chest. The action wrenched his insides, and a truth came to him in that moment that he hadn't recognized for eight years. He'd missed her. He'd missed her horribly.

He'd missed her closeness, that touching and holding. Yet he'd never let himself feel that until right then or let himself admit that he'd missed the feel of her and the scent of her. Despite the circumstances, he could feel his whole being responding to the soft sigh that escaped her lips and the way she snuggled into him. He cut off his responses any way he could, and that meant facing the fact that she'd fainted because she'd found out their marriage had never been annulled.

That brought a coldness to his spirit, and he moved abruptly, standing once again with her in his arms. He headed over to the elevator, where the doors still stood open. He went inside, shifted her to touch the button for the top floor, then stood back as the elevator started up.

She shifted in his hold again to settle into his arms, and he could feel his breath catch in his chest. He'd held her like this before, going into the hotel room in Nevada. Married. He'd thought it had been for twenty-four hours, and it had turned out to be for eight years.

The thought settled into him, not with the same horror it obviously had with Candice, but with a sense of sorrow that their marriage hadn't been based on love. It might have survived if it had been. She might have come with him to Dallas and forgotten all about her family and what they'd wanted for her.

"Married," he murmured, his voice softly echoing in the close confines. "I'll be damned."

"Mmm," Candice breathed as she pressed a hand to his chest just above his heart.

He closed his eyes tightly, the sensations coursing through him scattered and tense. He responded to her in his arms, and he hurt from the thought that the idea of marriage to him was still frightening to her. He was very thankful when the doors opened and he stepped out onto the top floor of the hotel. Then he realized that he had no idea what room Sandi was in, much less a key. He looked up and down the broad, beige-on-beige corridor, then knew he didn't have a choice.

He wasn't about to embarrass Candice, and the only place he could take her that wouldn't be over-run with guests was his room one floor down. He stepped back into the elevator, pushed the button for his floor, and as the doors slid shut, he wondered if he was quite mad. The thing to do was to get as far away from Candice as he could until he could sort this all out. Instead, he was taking her to his hotel room.

The elevator stopped, the doors opened and he hesitated for a moment, but finally knew he had no choice. He stepped into the deserted hallway and headed for his suite at the far end. He fumbled with one hand to get the key card out of his pocket, but couldn't manage to get to his pocket with her pressed against him.

Carefully he shifted her back, then over his shoulder, the way he had carried her on the beach. He'd done it that time to annoy her and she'd fought. But this time she wasn't fighting. Her one arm actually entwined with his arm, and she was making those soft sighing noises that were playing havoc with him. He got out the key as quickly as he could, slipped it into the slot on the door lock and clicked the door open to step into the shadowed room.

He crossed the sitting area, headed to the huge bed near the windows and eased her down onto the muted spread. She sighed, rolled onto her side, and her hands slipped under her cheek.

God, she really was beautiful, he thought, staring down at her in the soft shadows. His wife. The thought was there and unavoidable. She was his wife, and she was going to marry Mark. That thought twisted inside of him. He stood very still, forcing himself not to touch her again. His control only extended so far. But nothing was stopping an aching need for the woman in his bed. An aching need for the woman who had been his wife for eight years.

Candice came out of one softness into more softness, to a place she couldn't remember ever being. Coolness under her, soft comfort, then memory came in floating shards. Shimmering memories of falling, being caught and held, cradled in strong arms and carried. J.T. It had been him. She stirred, turning, and, as she opened her eyes, he was there, standing over her, part of the shadows that fell behind him.

It was like a dream, a dream she'd had before. A dream that had come over and over again through the years. J.T. by her, close, yet when she reached out, there would be nothing. J.T. would turn away from her, out of her reach, and leave her alone. There'd be a certain sadness, mingling with an odd pain that lasted until she woke and put it all behind her.

But this time was different. When she reached out, she felt him. His hand, she thought, as his fingers laced with hers. She'd done it this time. She'd touched him, and the loneliness was being pushed back farther and farther as he came down to her, then over her. She felt heat instead of coldness and a sense of where she'd wanted to be forever settled over her.

The dream was so real, she could feel J.T. coming toward her, stirring the air, then he was against her, his body along hers and his lips found hers. The contact was a flash of fire, an explosion of need that was achingly overwhelming and infinitely familiar. His mouth claimed hers, his exploration of hers urgent, and the hunger between them was almost painful.

She felt everything in exquisite detail. His tongue touched hers, then skimmed over her lips, tracing along her tongue to invade her depths. His hand feathered along her bare arm, then around to her exposed stomach. The contact of skin on skin was searing, making her tremble and all reason flee. She arched toward him, memories of the past flooding over her, him touching her, kissing her, claiming her. That first time. The very first time for everything for her. And she ached to know it again.

As she strained to get closer, she knew this was no dream. His hands were on her, sliding under the clinging material of her top, and the skin on skin was a burning reality. Her flimsy bra was gone, pushed aside, and his hand found her breasts, catching at her nipple, and an ache built in her that rose to fierce heights. She heard soft moans and knew it was her, accepting that making love with J.T. was more than a dream that had haunted her for eight years. It was becoming reality.

If she let go, if she gave in to every need inside her, she could have it again. She could know the heights, the glory, and a release that had frightened her at the same time it had brought incredible peace to her. His lips found her throat, the pulse that beat frantically there, then trailed down to the hollow, lower, to bunched material pulled up to expose her breasts.

The sound of tearing material was there, then she was free of the top, and his lips found her breast. His tongue teased her nipple, drawing whimpering sounds from her, and building a knot in her that screamed for release. His touch spanned her diaphragm, then slipped lower, with the tips of his fingers at the waist of the skirt. As they slipped under the waistband, she felt him pressing against her, felt his arousal against her thigh, and she wanted nothing more than to give in and let him make love to her.

All of a sudden, grim reality was there between them. He didn't love her. He'd never loved her. He'd never said he loved her. They'd had sex. They'd never made love. That was why it had been so wrong. He'd only wanted her, and he obviously wanted her again. She felt his hot breath on her skin, and felt the urgency in his touch. She knew she could have it all again, but she would end up the same way—in pain and faced with the task of rebuilding whatever she had left of her life.

She couldn't do that again. She wasn't sure she could even live through it again, not now when she knew how perverse her response was to him. It was strong, painfully strong. And wrong. She twisted away from him, jerking free, and scooted to the farthest side of the bed. She struggled to sit up, felt the light-headedness again for a moment, then braced herself with one hand and pushed. She clutched at the ruined material of her top, holding it together across her tender breasts.

It was then that she realized she didn't even know where she was. She was sitting on the far side of a huge bed, across from J.T., but even with the dim light, she knew this wasn't Sandi's suite. This place was larger, dominated by the bed and a huge armoire on one wall. An armoire that had something hanging from a partially open side door. Then she saw what hung in the shadows. A dress. A long dress.

It was J.T.'s room, J.T.'s and Vonya's, and she swallowed quickly to stop sickness that churned in her middle. "What are you doing?" she breathed, fighting the urge to scrub her hand across her lips.

"It's called a kiss," he said from behind her, but thankfully at a distance.

A simple word for something that had the potential to ruin everything. "I meant…" She closed her eyes tightly. "How did I get here?"

"Do you want the stork story or the truth?"

That did it. Anger flared in her and she swung off the bed, onto the floor and the bruise on the bottom of her foot shot pain up her leg. She grabbed for the support of the bedpost, then turned to face J.T. Thankfully, he was on the far side of the bed, his expression touched by shadows, and she didn't even look at the way the comforter was mussed. "You know what I'm talking about. Here. This room. It's your room, yours and that model's, isn't it?"

"It was either bring you here or walk through the lobby with you to find Sandi and get her room key, then carry you up here." He chuckled, a humorless sound that made her sickness increase. "Darlin', I knew you didn't want to be seen like that. So, I carried you up here…" He hesitated, then added, "Over my shoulder."

That teasing, even through the shadows, was cutting away at the heat and need in her that was making her tremble. "Over your shoulder?" She remembered, all too well, the walk on the beach.

He slipped off his jacket and tossed it onto the bed between them. "I couldn't get my key out of my pocket, so I had to improvise, and that meant I had to—"

She held out one hand to him palm out. "Spare me the details. Just tell me that no one saw us." She looked around. "And that that woman isn't somewhere around here."

He tugged at his tie and unfurled it, leaving it hanging around his neck while he unsnapped the cummerbund and tossed it over the jacket. "Relax, Vonya isn't here, and no one saw us, either," he muttered. "Not even your fiancé."

Fiancé? Oh, that brought back a world of trouble. A fiancé when she was still married to another man? She didn't even know if that could happen. "Was I..." She touched her tongue to remarkably cold lips. "Tell me I was hallucinating down there."

"You passed out, you didn't see little green men," he said, unsnapping his cuff links.

"That isn't what I meant."

"Of course you didn't," he said softly with that drawl, and turned away from her, sitting on the bed while he casually took off his shoes. "Absolutely ruined," he murmured as he tossed them one at a time into the shadows, the dull thuds echoing in the room. "There was no annulment."

The words stood between them. "J.T., I really thought you'd taken care of it. I never would have—"

"No, you wouldn't have, would you?" he said. "And now you want to marry Forester. I'd say you've got a mess on your hands, darlin'."

She stood very still, watching, almost afraid when he started to shrug out of his shirt. Then the shirt was gone and she could see his strong back, the way the muscles flexed as he sat forward, then he stood. But he didn't turn. He walked across into the deeper shadows, and she realized he was heading for the small bar by the shuttered windows when he asked over his shoulder, "Drink?"

She wished she could drink and make this all go away, but none of it was going away. Not even the way her mouth went dry at the sight of J.T. half-dressed, casually splashing something into a glass. Then he turned and held up the glass in her direction. "Well?"

"No," she said, then he was coming across to her.

He didn't let the bed stay between them this time, coming around the footboard. He stopped with two feet separating them. "You look terrified," he commented almost angrily, before he tossed most of the drink to the back of his throat.

"I never dreamed..." Her voice trailed off. Oh, she'd dreamed a lot, but nothing that she'd ever tell him. Never would he know that those dreams had held the fantasy of him coming for her eight years ago and sweeping her away. Taking any decision out of her hands. Riding off into the sunset like every romantic cowboy. If she hadn't felt so tense right then, she would have laughed at the idea. Riding off into the sunset with a cowboy. No, it wasn't funny. Not when J.T. was that cowboy.

"No, you didn't," he murmured, then held out his free hand, touching her chin lightly, and she froze. "Hey, relax. This is no big thing." His touch on her was gone, and he finished the last of his drink. "We'll just get the annulment. Finally." He watched her narrowly as he gripped the empty glass. "No one will ever have to know. I promise."

Words she wanted to hear settled around her, and she couldn't begin to understand why they made her feel so sad. "Thank you," she made herself say.

She wasn't prepared for the way J.T. reached out to her again, tapped the tip of her nose gently and said, "Just an early wedding present for you and Mark."

J.T. knew his words sounded casually magnanimous, but they hid his thoughts completely. He was close, too close to Candice, and he knew he shouldn't touch her, even a slight contact on the nose. The words hid that lingering ache of need and any foolishness that had grown with their connection on the bed.

He was thankful he was leaving for London later that night. He needed distance, and he knew that sanity would come back to him when Candice wasn't within easy reach. God, his hormones were playing havoc with him, just the way they had eight years ago, or he'd never have taken her across the state line to get married.

He stared hard at her, her features blurred slightly by the shadows of the room, and the truth of the piece of paper in his pocket hit him hard. If there had been love, there would have been no thought of annulment. It would have been what he'd wanted back then, to have her forever. That truth had been hidden securely in the past, under layers of denial, layers of foolishness.

Her tongue touched her lips, and he knew that if anyone was made to be loved, it was Candice. To be loved often and well. He just wished that he was the man she'd chosen, that he wasn't the man she'd walked away from. He inhaled, taking in that gentle scent of sweetness that seemed to permeate the world around Candice, not aware she'd spoken until she repeated herself.

"Do you mean that?" Her voice coursed through him, even though it was barely above a whisper.

"Mean what?" He couldn't even remember what had been said.

He was very aware of the way she was clutching her top closed, the way her teeth nibbled her full lip. "We…we can get this over with?"

"Of course." He sounded reasonable, even though he was fighting an overwhelming urge to hold on to her again. "We can get this finished."

She shrugged, a fluttery, vulnerable motion that really touched him. Hell, he felt protective of her, wishing he had the right to hold on to her again, to support her and shelter her from all the ugliness that permeated the world. Nothing that she'd want him to do, that was for sure. "Okay, then we…we just get the annulment and then…"

"It's over," he said, hating those words.

She shifted from foot to foot, obviously nervous and anxious. "I'll have my attorney contact yours and take care of everything."

"Okay. I'll be in London for a few days, but I'll be back in Dallas by the end of next week. Have your attorney send the papers to Davis, my assistant, at my main offices. Davis is discreet and he'll take care of everything.'' God, he sounded as if he was dissolving a company. Cold and clinical. But it felt anything but cold and clinical to him.

"Okay, sure, we can do this quietly and just get it over with.'' She was speaking faster now. "I'll tell my attorney to only deal with Davis.''

He could see the relief flood through her and it hurt like hell, even though he was eight years late in doing what he should have done. Candice had Mark, and she wanted her life. He'd give it to her. "You never said if you'd told your fiancé about…all of this,'' he said, the words coming before he knew he was going to say them.

She shook her head. "No, I mean, we don't feel the need to tell each other about our…our past involvements.''

"How about past marriages?'' he asked more bluntly than he'd intended to.

She lifted her chin a bit, the way her mother did when she was about to assert the Montgomery supremacy. An action he'd always hated…until Candice did it. It was endearing on some level with her, almost amusing. Almost. "There wasn't a real marriage, so I don't see how—''

"We got married. We took off, crossed the border, found a justice of the peace in Nevada, got married and didn't spend the night playing tiddly-winks.'' He wished he could take that edge out of his voice. "But it's up to you if you tell Mark the truth or not. It's nothing to me.''

"Exactly,'' she murmured, then moved abruptly, skirting around him, limping noticeably on her sore foot. She didn't touch him, but definitely stirred the air around him. "And it's nothing to me what you told the model, or is it, your filly?"

He didn't turn. "Vonya. And I wouldn't do that if I were you."

"Do what?"

"Walk out of this room half-naked."

Candice stopped dead in her tracks, her sore foot hovering just above the carpeted floor and her hand touching the door for balance. She'd been so distracted by J.T. and getting away from him, she hadn't even been thinking about what she looked like.

She looked down at her ruined dress, at the top that had been torn jaggedly down the front, and she knew he was right. Thankfully, when she looked back at J.T., he wasn't smiling. She couldn't have dealt with that. This just went from bad to worse. "You tore it."

"Sorry," he said, not sounding sorry at all. "But if you care at all about what people say, I wouldn't walk out of here in a robe, either."

"You did it, you tell me what to do," she said, grabbing at some indignation, but unable to find it in herself. She just felt sick.

He crossed to the armoire, swung open the other door to show a line of drawers and opened the top one. He took something out and turned to her. All she saw was something folded in his hands, but it made her swallow again to get out her words. "Oh no, not that," she said, the idea of wearing something that Vonya had worn making her nauseated. "I'm not wearing your girlfriend's clothes."

The idea was sudden and devastating, that she'd been in their bed with J.T., almost offering herself to him. The sickness grew in leaps and bounds. She hated herself at that moment, and wished that she hated him.

J.T. was in front of her, and he shook out a long-sleeved, chambray shirt. "It's mine. Vonya never unpacked. Take off your top and put this on."

She looked at the shirt in his hands, then slowly took it. "Thanks," she muttered, but didn't do what he said. Instead, she slipped on the shirt over her ruined clothes, the sleeves falling to her fingertips and the tail partway down her thighs. But it covered her. With awkward fingers, she fumbled with the buttons and did them up.

She thought the shirt would be better than Vonya's clothing, but she hadn't counted on the soft cotton feeling like J.T. She didn't know where that thought came from, then realized it was from the past, from a moment in time when she'd slipped on one of his shirts after making love. She trembled slightly, and covered it with a forced cough to clear her throat. "I need to get going."

"Candice?"

She looked up at him. "What?"

He hesitated, then said, "Davis, have your attorney contact Davis."

"Yes, of course," she said and turned, reaching for the doorknob. In a heartbeat she was out in the corridor and the door was closing behind her. J.T. was safely behind the barrier, and she was alone. She stood there, leaning against the wall while she caught her breath and pressed her hand to her middle.

She closed her eyes tightly and flinched when she

heard a dull thud coming from behind the closed door.

"We didn't spend the night playing tiddlywinks."

His words rang in her mind, bringing unwanted heat to her being. No, they'd had sex. That was one thing they had done well for a single night. She took a shaky breath, straightened, then limped toward the elevators at the far end of the corridor. She wouldn't let herself think about that one night. A night that could have been repeated if she'd given in to her needs just moments ago.

She never learned. Some things never changed. One touch and she'd crumpled into his arms. She could feel the clinging saltwater on her skin, and the softness of the shirt brushing against her skin as she made her way to the elevators. It wasn't until she was at the elevator doors that she finally realized she'd forgotten her shoes. She stopped, but didn't turn to look back. No, she had no idea where they were. Down on the beach? Did J.T. have them? She wasn't going back. She had more shoes in Sandi's room.

Reaching out to push the floor button, she ignored the unsteadiness in her hand before she drew it back and curled it into a fist by her side. She took another tight breath as she waited for the elevator and tried not to look at her blurred reflection in the closed doors. Death warmed over would have been an improvement, all in an oversize blue shirt. Even in the poor reflection, she could tell she looked pale. Thank God they hadn't run into anyone, she thought.

But that relief was shattered when the elevator doors opened and she stood face-to-face with Mark, a perfectly groomed Mark, who was looking at her with shock and horror.

Chapter Seven

"My God, what happened to you?" Mark asked.

Candice pushed past him into the elevator car, not giving him a chance to get out, and she grabbed at the railing along the mirrored wall. Mirrors. She deliberately kept from looking at a clear vision of herself. Instead, she hit the button for the top floor and leaned back against the cold wall. She looked at Mark as the doors slid shut.

"Mark, I can explain." She took a sharp breath, trying to ease a tightness in her chest as he stared at her.

"I hope so. You were gone. I went looking for you, and someone said you were on the beach, then a bellhop said he saw a woman from the wedding being carried over a man's shoulders along the beach."

If she could have groaned, she would have. But there was no air in her lungs right then.

"Was that you? And what in the hell happened to your clothes?" He came closer and touched the collar of J.T.'s shirt. "Where did you get this?"

She bit her lip hard and felt as if she were standing in front of her father, trying to find an explanation that would take away his censure. She hated that feeling, but she knew that she owed Mark an explanation, one way or another. "Just slow down. I can explain. I was on the beach and…" She couldn't figure out what to say without mentioning J.T., and she didn't want to do that.

The elevator stopped and the doors opened, giving her a reprieve of sorts, and she took one step toward the opening. But she didn't make her escape. Mark stopped her from getting out, holding the door open with one hand and touching her shoulder with the other.

"You're limping, and you're wearing a man's shirt. I think I deserve an explanation."

There was a tinge of anger now that had little to do with concern. Candice could barely stand to look at him. "My foot. I think I bruised it." She stuck to the truth as much as she could and prayed that Mark wouldn't ask anything about the man carrying her on the beach. "I went down to the beach, fell off the rocks into a tide pool and stepped on a sharp stone. My foot is really sore. Probably a bruise."

"And the shirt?" he asked, his expression tight. "Your dress is ruined, too."

"The water ruined it," she said, then shrugged away from his touch. "And I need to change."

She moved away from him and out into the corridor, not looking back to see if Mark was following her or not. She just wanted to go to Sandi's room, get changed and forget about everything.

She reached Sandi's door, then realized she had no way to get inside the suite. The key was downstairs with either Sandi or Steffi, and she was stuck. She turned, and Mark was there, blocking her path back to the elevator. He came closer still, flicking at the hair clinging to her face. She flinched at the contact. One thing she knew, though, was she didn't want to be touched by anyone right now.

"Mark, I'm sorry about all of this. I didn't plan it. It was an accident, and I'm too worn out by everything to go into some long explanation. I just need to get into Sandi's room to get my clothes and clean up."

He drew back from her and asked her something she never saw coming. "If you were coming to Sandi's room, what were you doing on the floor below?"

She couldn't believe this was happening. She wasn't good at lying, and she didn't want to feel angry at Mark for cornering her, but she did. "Just leave it alone," she muttered.

"You got off at the wrong floor?" he asked, giving her a perfect explanation.

"Yes, sure," she murmured. Wrong floor, wrong man, wrong thing to do.

"Thank God your mother can't see you," he stressed. "She barely got over the bare middle and the bare feet at the service."

She halfway expected his face to show that he was teasing. But there wasn't a trace of humor there. Just dead earnestness. He wasn't like J.T. at all. Why was she comparing Mark to J.T.? No, she wasn't about to start that, not when it would come full circle to those few moments in J.T.'s room.

"Of course not," she said softly, hating the unsteadiness in her hands and the growing anger in her that had no real target beyond herself. "What am I going to do? I forgot that I don't have a room key."

She leaned back against the wall and exhaled. ''This wasn't in the plan.''

Not much of what had happened tonight had been in any of her plans, starting with the wedding and ending with letting J.T. kiss her. No, she'd kissed him. She couldn't blame that on him alone. Not any more than she could blame the fact that they were still married on him. If she hadn't been so anxious to forget the hurt and the stupidity of the elopement, she would have made sure the marriage was over. But she hadn't.

''My room.''

She didn't understand. ''What?''

He laughed softly, leaning toward her, his whole demeanor changing. ''Don't look so shocked. We're engaged.'' His finger touched her cheek and trailed along her jawline to her chin. ''And you look pretty cute, actually.''

She couldn't deal with this now, not with everything that had happened. And part of her wanted to be free of her ties with J.T. before going any further with Mark. ''We…we can't stay away from the party any longer.''

''Hey, it was just an idea. You can change and we can go back down. Or…'' His finger tapped her chin. ''It's up to you.''

''I…I need to change, and my clothes…'' She looked longingly at the locked door to Sandi's room. Nothing was going right, and she just wanted one damn thing to go right. That hadn't actually been a prayer, but whatever it was, it was answered when the elevator doors opened and Sandi's sister, Steffi, stepped off.

She came down the hall and Mark moved back

as she came close enough to realize who was outside the door. "Candice...Mark? What's going on?" Her eyes widened on Candice. "My God, what did he do to you and why are you wearing his shirt?"

"Absolutely nothing. I fell on the beach, got wet, and a man offered me this shirt." That was the truth, and a relief to get past it. "I need to change."

Steffi pushed between the two of them, to slip the key card into the slot, then click open the door. "I'll say you do." She looked at Mark. "Why don't you go on down and get yourself a drink. I'll take care of Candice, and we'll be down in time for the bouquet toss."

Mark hesitated, then bent to kiss Candice on the cheek before he backed up. "I'll see you downstairs." Then he turned and headed back down the hallway.

Candice hurried into the suite, thankful to have Mark gone for now, and spoke quickly, "Thank goodness you showed up. This dress is ruined and I need my clothes."

"You're limping," Steffi said, leading the way across the sitting area to the bedroom area.

"I stepped on a stone. I bruised my foot." She limped after Steffi and into a huge dressing area off the bath and bedroom. When Steffi turned on the overhead lights, Candice was relieved to see her clothes hanging in the side closet. "I can't believe this happened."

"How did you fall?" Steffi asked as she held out a towel to Candice. "You've got dirt on your face."

She crossed to reach for the towel and went into where a double vanity ran the length of one wall in the bathroom. "I lost my footing on the side of a tide pool,'' she said over her shoulder. She tossed the towel on the vanity, then reached to turn on the lights. The moment she saw herself in the mirrors, she wished the world was black and no light existed.

Any reflection she'd seen earlier didn't do her justice. A drowned rat? Death warmed over? Very mild descriptions. Dirt streaked across her cheek, her hair was flat and clinging to her head, and any makeup she might have had to begin with was gone. She turned on the water in the nearest sink, cupped the coolness in her hands and splashed it on her face.

''So, what was going on that you were on the beach?''

''Just walking,'' she said as she reached for the towel.

''With J.T.?''

The question jolted her and the towel tumbled from her hands onto the sink. Quickly, she reached for it again and pressed it to her face while she tried to gather her wits about her. ''I'm sorry,'' she said as she dropped the towel in a heap by the sink, then started fiddling with her hair. ''I'm sorry, what did you say?''

''J.T. I saw you leave with him. I just assumed he was there when you fell.'' Candice looked at Steffi in the mirror. ''I figured it was his shirt, but I wasn't going to say anything in front of Mark.''

Candice closed her eyes for a moment, then opened them and spotted a brush on the vanity. She reached for it and started to tug it through her hair, grimacing as it made her eyes smart and water. ''He was getting some air, too,'' she said, totally ignoring the shirt observation.

"What is it with the two of you?" Steffi asked, that question as jarring as the first.

Candice intently fussed with her hair, staring hard at herself in the mirror as she tugged the brush through it. "What are you talking about?" she asked, trying to be casual.

"You and J.T., you both act like you're walking on eggshells around each other. There's tension there. I just didn't know why."

Candice had thought no one noticed, and she'd been wrong, as wrong as she'd been about so many things today. She tried to think of what to say. "There's...there's nothing." The lie all but choked her. "I knew J.T. years ago, but he hasn't been back here for...for a long time. He's Dylan's friend."

"Why wasn't he here for Dylan's wedding?" Steffi came into the room and leaned against the wall by the towel racks.

"I don't know. I don't know much about J.T. anymore." She looked around for the hotel toiletries and took out a small bottle of hair spray. She'd managed to get her hair relatively smooth, and she sprayed it to make sure it didn't start to curl. "Why don't you ask him."

Her tone must have held an edge, because Steffi frowned and said, "Sorry, I didn't mean to be nosy."

Candice turned to Steffi, worn out trying to deal with everything. "No, I'm sorry. I've been a bit on edge all day. I didn't expect all of this when I came back, and I'm worried about Dylan and Whitney stranded like that." She shrugged and walked toward Steffi and the door. "I just don't know much about J.T. or what he's doing or what he isn't doing.''

''You know, if I wasn't married, J.T. Watson looks pretty damn sexy to me.''

He'd always been pretty damn sexy. That's what had caused her downfall eight years ago, and what had almost been her downfall tonight. ''I guess so,'' she murmured as she brushed past Steffi. She stripped off J.T.'s shirt, tossing it onto the floor, and ignored Steffi's slight gasp when she saw just how ruined the dress was.

''My God, it's a mess.'' She shook her head. ''It's ruined.''

The top hung limply on her and was easy to shrug out of and toss on top of J.T.'s shirt. Then she tried to unzip the skirt, but her fingers tugged futilely at it. Steffi was there, tugging at it with her, and it gave way, finally, falling around her ankles.

She stepped over the ruined fabric and crossed to where her dress hung, a simple cream-colored silk shift, with a cocktail-length skirt and a softly dipped neckline. *Simple and elegant,* her mother had said when she'd bought it a few weeks ago. *Understated and timeless.* Something that would have been wonderful on Grace Montgomery, matching the woman herself, with her elegance and timelessness.

''I'll never understand why he never got married,'' Steffi was saying as she nudged the damaged skirt farther from them with the toe of her gold pump. ''J.T. Watson is sexy as hell in a tux, and in those jeans he wears, well...'' She exhaled an exaggerated sigh. ''Whew, cowboys do it for me.''

''He's hardly a cowboy,'' Candice commented as she slipped the soft silk over her head and let it fall around her. "He's the head of one of the largest corporations in the country."

"Sure, that's what he does. I'm talking about what he is. Jack told me the guy's got a huge spread in Texas, rides a horse like he was born to it, wears a Stetson with those sexy jeans, and he even cooks. Probably buffalo."

No, just simple food, like steaks. Candice was shocked that she not only remembered that meal he'd cooked for her so long ago on the terrace of the guest house on the estate, but that she could almost smell the charcoal and meat scents. *"A real old-fashioned barbecue,"* he'd said.

She quickly smoothed the silk at her hips, then reached for the matching ivory heels she'd worn to the hotel. "He sounds perfect," she said, sinking onto the nearby chair.

"Obviously. Now, that brings up an obvious question."

Candice looked up at Steffi as she slipped on one shoe then reached for the other. "It does?"

"Why isn't he married?"

Candice grimaced in pain while trying to put the shoe on her sore foot, but used the pain to cover any reaction she had to Steffi's question. It didn't hit her until then that either one of them could have remarried at anytime in the last eight years and never known it was illegal. "He never got married?" she asked, taking off both shoes and standing in her bare feet.

"Never. And I know he likes women. From what I've heard, he's had his share of them. And that Vonya that he brought, well, she's not chopped meat."

She thought of the room down one floor, their room, and that brought a sudden and violent surge of sickness to Candice. She moved quickly to cover, grabbing at her reality. "Mark's waiting. I need to get downstairs."

"Mark Forester isn't hard to look at," Steffi said. "No cowboy, but not bad. I'm sure he's had his share of gorgeous women." She grinned. "Look at who he's going to marry. And, by the way, when are you going to decide on the date?"

Candice had never realized what a talker Steffi was, or that the woman had the power to ask questions that kept Candice's world teetering. "We decided on Labor Day weekend."

"Oh, wow, that's terrific," Steffi all but squealed. "No one told me."

"Because we haven't told anyone yet. We just decided tonight."

"It's this wedding thing," Steffi said with a sigh. "It brings out the romance in everyone." She clasped her hands together in delight. "Now that you've decided, you'll be having parties and, of course, there's the reception—"

Candice couldn't bear to think of celebrating her marriage to Mark, not when she was still legally married to J.T. "I'll call you when we decide what we're doing," she said. "I promise."

"I'm sorry. That's the problem with being a wedding coordinator. I'm always thinking about business," she said with obvious embarrassment. "It's a bad habit of mine."

"Don't worry, I'm used to it," Candice said, sobering. "I was brought up that way."

"I bet your father would be thrilled to have a man like Mark as a son-in-law."

Candice tossed her shoes on the floor, and knew that Steffi was absolutely right. Her father would have approved wholeheartedly of Mark. "Yes, he would have been pleased," she murmured, then stood. "I can't get my shoes on, so I guess I'll have to go barefoot a bit longer."

"You know," Steffi said as she studied Candice, "Sandi thought you'd wig out over the dress, and then about going barefoot, but I told her you weren't nearly as uptight as she thinks you are."

"Thanks, I guess," she said in disbelief.

"Oh, no offense meant. It's just, you're a Montgomery. The founding family. And you've always had this...air about you." She grinned at Candice's bare feet. "Who would have thought you'd be suggesting going barefoot again?"

"I hurt my foot," she said, hating the idea that people thought she was so arrogant. "I don't have a choice, and barefoot is better than killing myself forcing on the shoe." She motioned to the door. "Now, are you coming?"

She glanced at her watch. "Whoa, I told Sandi I'd be right back. I just came up for my camera. I haven't gotten one single picture yet." She crossed to a shelf by the bathroom door, grabbed a leather case and came back to follow Candice into the hallway.

The door clicked shut behind them, and Candice was thankful for the soft carpeting as they headed for the elevators.

"I'll have to make very sure I get one of you and Mark." Steffi stopped by the elevators and pressed the down button before she turned to Candice with a grin. "You'll have to have something to commemorate today so you'll remember it forever."

Candice doubted she'd ever forget this day, with or without a picture, and she was saved from having to say a hollow thank-you when the elevator doors opened. They got inside and as the doors shut, Candice looked at Steffi. "Can I ask you something?"

"Sure, fire away."

"Do you really think I'm a snob?"

She grinned again. "Snob? A bit…oh, how can I say this? A bit upper-class, maybe stuffy." She motioned at her dress, the duplicate of the one Candice had ruined. "You should have seen your face when Sandi showed you the dresses, then told you that you were going barefoot."

"I was surprised. I expected blue satin or pink silk, not that amber, clingy, half-not-there stuff. And if she'd put a temporary floor on the sand, we could have worn our shoes."

"See? You would have put down the floor, wouldn't you?"

"Of course."

"And worn shoes?"

"Of course."

"And the dress would have been long and elegant and something in ivory silk?"

"I guess so."

"And you would have married Mark in a very formal ceremony. None of that off-the-cuff, spur-of-the-moment, let-it-all-hang-out sort of ceremony, right?"

All she could manage was a nod as images from a marriage that had been off-the-cuff, spur-of-the-moment came to her with a clarity that made her chest tighten.

"So, he's perfect for you. The same family types, the same sense of manners and rightness." She grinned. "He's no cowboy, that's for sure."

Her chest tightened. "What makes you say that?"

The doors opened, but Steffi didn't get out right away. She shrugged. "If he were a cowboy, you'd never look at him, much less marry him. Can you imagine what would happen if you did?"

That made Candice feel sick, almost as sick as the idea of eight years of being married and never knowing it. She cut off Steffi's words by quickly getting out of the elevator and heading away from the woman. But that didn't stop her. Steffi was right beside her on the way to the ballroom. "Hey, I'm sorry. I didn't mean to put anyone down, especially someone like J.T. I just meant that you have your place and you know it."

"My place?" she asked in a tight voice as she continued to walk swiftly toward the arched entry to the ballroom. "My place?"

"I did it again, didn't I? I just meant, you're a Montgomery. Everyone knows what that means."

Candice stopped at the entry, the sickness morphing into a heaviness that seemed to be pressing down on her. "Well, I'm glad everyone does, because I don't," she said, trying—and failing—to keep the hurt out of her voice.

With that, she turned from Steffi and went through the doors into the cavernous room. She wasn't aware of anything except Vonya nearby, smiling and talking to some of the guests. Tall and gorgeous. One of J.T.'s women. One of probably a lot of women.

Suddenly she sensed something coming toward her through the air. Instinctively, she put up her hands, and as a cheer went up from the guests, she looked down at a bouquet of white roses and baby breath woven with gold ribbons. She stared at what she was holding. She'd caught the bridal bouquet.

She looked up and Vonya was there, clapping and smiling. "Great catch," she said. "You're going to be the next bride."

Candice stared at Vonya, then down at the flowers she was all but crushing in her hold. Bride? She could have said she'd just caught the plague and Candice couldn't have felt worse. She swallowed hard, tried to smile, but all attempts at a smile died when she looked up and saw J.T. directly across from her. He'd changed into a white, band-collared shirt, tight jeans and his boots.

"J.T. Watson is sexy as hell in a tux, and in those jeans he wears, well..." Steffi had said. Only the Stetson was missing.

Those hazel eyes flicked from Vonya to her as a slow, easy smile edged with obvious delight at her discomfort sent her reeling.

"If he were a cowboy, you'd never look at him, much less marry him."

He lifted a champagne glass in her direction. She didn't have to be able to hear him to know that he said, "To your wedding."

"...you have your place and you know it."

She could feel her knees buckling, but thankfully Mark was there, laughing and clapping, and saying, "What a coincidence." His hold on her was all that kept her from collapsing as she fought to shut out J.T. and that smile. Along with the painfully fresh memory of being with him in his room, and the fact that he was still her husband. A husband who had never loved her.

Chapter Eight

J.T. was watching Vonya across the ballroom, wondering how he could look at her and think in any terms but passion. But he was. She was beautiful, fitting in with the guests with ease and grace, taking the time to spot him and smile and wave. Yet he could appreciate her, even enjoy looking at her, but still he was thankful they were leaving as soon as the wedding was over. She'd go to Saint Tropez and he'd go back to London. No regrets that there hadn't been more.

Then Candice was there, stepping into the room. And every bit of passion and desire that he should have felt for Vonya, he felt for the delicate blond woman, his wife of eight years.

She'd changed into a simple dress, certainly not a sexy one. Her hair was smoothed back from her exquisitely lovely face, and her feet were still bare. Right at that moment, Sandi sent the bridal bouquet flying through the air in a high arch in the direction of the group of women by the entry.

The action ground into slow motion for him, Candice looking up, seeing the bouquet, then her hands lifting almost self-protectively, catching the white and gold bundle. Deep blue eyes were wide with shock, and her pale lips formed an *O* as the clapping and laughing started up.

Then things happened quickly, perversely rushing past him. Candice looking over at him, high color touching her cheeks, a salute that he didn't know he was going to do until it was done, then Mark was there. The man was close to her, his hands touching her, and she was moving toward him, into his hold.

J.T. turned away, finished off his drink and ignored the laughter and clapping behind him. It was a new experience for J.T. to feel confused, but that's just how he felt. The confusion had been there since his first glimpse of Candice in the wedding party, but had taken on a life of its own when he'd kissed her in his room.

How could he hate a man he didn't even really know? How could he still want a woman who wanted another man? Everything about Candice in his life had defied logic and reason. Especially his reactions to her.

"So, you have forgone the tuxedo for more comfortable clothes?"

J.T. turned and Karl was there, the gray-haired man studying him with that look. He'd just bet that the man knew the tuxedo hadn't been taken off for comfort. But he was being polite, giving J.T. a chance to explain why he wasn't wearing it any longer. He liked this man.

"Do you want the truth or do you want me to spare your feelings?"

Karl smiled at him, his gray mustache twitching with the expression. "I believe that the truth is always the best route, although one is not always able to practice that in its purest sense.''

J.T. smiled at the man. He didn't know Karl very well, but on some basic level, he felt a connection with him. That hadn't happened to J.T. too often in this life, but for some reason it was happening now with a man who was old enough to be his father. ''I had an unfortunate experience with the ocean, and I really didn't want to wear the tuxedo the way it looked. It would have done a disservice to you and your artistry.''

J.T.'s admiration of the man increased when Karl didn't appear shocked or outraged. Instead, his smile turned a bit wry, accompanied by a slight shake of his head. ''Well, my boy, it was yours, yours to swim in, if that was what you wished to do.''

There was no prima donna act, no artist with a temperament who would be angered at the destruction of his work, but a definite sense of humor. ''Let me assure you that the jacket is just fine. It survived, but the pants won't be seeing the light of day again.''

''Is that why you look so deep in thought when everyone else is having a glorious time? You were pondering the fate of the tuxedo?'' He waved his hand dismissively. ''You have my permission to throw it out with a clear conscience.''

''Thanks for that, but I was trying to figure out what to do about something else in my life.''

''A problem?''

''I don't know,'' he said, but realized what a lie that evasion was. ''A surprise complication.''

''From what I have been told, you solve major

problems before breakfast. This one must be of great importance to you.''

He could hardly admit how important it was to figure out what was going on with him when Candice was around. ''It's bothersome, that's for sure.''

''Oh, I see.''

J.T. fingered his empty glass. ''You see what?''

''This sounds like woman trouble.''

J.T. had the distinct feeling again that Karl could read minds. A distinctly uncomfortable feeling. ''I need to go outside and get some fresh air.''

But before he could head for the open doors on the far side of the ballroom, Karl touched his shoulder. ''I just happen to have two of the best cigars known to mankind in my pocket. Would you do me the honor of sharing them with me?''

The old-worldly air about the man was in full force, and J.T. had the urge to bow before accepting the offer. Instead, he simply nodded. ''Thanks. The patio?''

''Perfect,'' Karl murmured and started across the room.

J.T. led the way across the room without glancing at the dance floor. He'd been vaguely aware of Candice and Mark heading in that direction, and he didn't want to look over there to verify it. He stepped onto the worn stone-paved patio at the center of the complex of shops, restaurants and the hotel, surprised to find the area all but deserted.

Karl walked with him in silence, the sounds of music from the reception drifting out into the balmy night. When they got to the spreading oak in the center of the plaza, J.T. motioned to the wrought-iron bench that circled the trunk. "How about here?"

"Perfect," Karl said as he moved to sit on the bench. When J.T. sat beside him, he heard the older man sigh as he settled. "A lovely night in every way," he murmured as he reached into his jacket and pulled out a slim case. He flicked it open to expose two cigars, which he held out to J.T.

He took one of the brown cylinders and sat forward, his forearms on his knees. While Karl lit his, J.T. fingered his, turning it around and around between his thumb and forefinger.

"They are much better if they are smoked," Karl said.

J.T. stared at the cigar between his fingers, then looked at the older man who was puffing quietly on his, twirling it slowly as he lit it evenly. He exhaled smoke into the night and held the case with a built-in lighter and clip to J.T. "Are you going to join me?"

J.T. used the clip, then lit the cigar, and as he exhaled the sweet smoke, he sat back. He seldom smoked, but the cigar was everything Karl had said. "Cuban?" he asked.

"Close. They come from a small supplier in that area. A very special blend." He rolled the cigar in his fingers. "One of life's small pleasures." Then he looked at J.T. through the drifting smoke. "I have been where you are."

"Excuse me?"

"Woman trouble. It is a universal condition when one decides to take that chance by falling in love."

Love? J.T. thought about that. He wasn't sure he even knew what love was, much less if he'd ever experienced it. But whatever had happened with Candice had come close. He knew that now. "You don't have to be in love to have trouble," he murmured.

"You think not?"

"Were you in love?"

"Were you?" he retorted softly, a question meeting a question.

J.T. took another pull on the cigar, then exhaled a halo of smoke into the night sky. "I don't know. How about you?"

"I was never married, so one has to wonder if it was love or not. With real love, there would not only be marriage, but a marriage that would be forever. With love, whatever happens is forever," Karl said.

J.T. looked at the man. "You read that note, didn't you?"

"Note?"

"The piece of paper you said fell out of my pocket, the one you gave back to me," he said, fingering the cigar.

"What did it say?"

"'*When there is love, you are married forever.*'" J.T. repeated.

"And?"

"And what?"

Karl took his time drawing on the cigar and exhaling before he answered that question. "Do you agree?"

"I don't know."

"And what are you going to do about it?"

"Do about it? What is there to do about it?"

"One would think that is obvious. Are you going to find out for yourself if that is true?"

What was going on? ''I don't know what you're talking about.''

''First one must be married, then one must figure out if that marriage was forged from love or from…'' He shrugged. ''Something else.''

''Like what?''

Karl laughed and touched J.T.'s shoulder with the hand that held the cigar. The glow was near J.T.'s face, the scent of the cigar strong and sure. ''Lust, need, convenience, parental pressure. The list is endless.'' His humorous tone faltered. ''Almost as endless as one's reasons for not marrying.''

J.T. didn't know where this was going, but he wasn't going to wait around to find out. It was too eerie the way this man obviously knew what he had no way of knowing. He stood, his cigar glowing in the night. ''You never said what your problem with a woman was all about.''

''Neither did you, sir.'' Karl stood, too. ''Let us just say that there are things I should have done that I can never do now. The time is past.'' He touched J.T. on the shoulder again. ''Don't live with regrets. Find out what is real and what is not, then you can go on with your life before it's too late.''

For a man who didn't suffer confusion easily, J.T. felt totally confused. He couldn't figure out what was going on, either with himself or Candice. Or this man. But one thing he knew, Candice was marrying Mark, and she couldn't until they weren't married. ''Sometimes we just have to walk away and let things go,'' he said.

''No regrets? Just leave?''

''What did you do?''

The man took his time drawing on the cigar, then

the smoke drifted up, haloing his head as he said words that were oddly tight. "Nothing. But do not use me as a role model. I have made many, many mistakes. I trust you will do better than I did."

J.T. could hear an edge of sadness in the man's voice and wondered what had happened to put it there. But before he could say anything, Karl motioned to the hotel.

"It is time to go back." That brought an odd, humorless chuckle. "Then again, can one ever go back?"

J.T. stared at the glow of lights spilling out into the night from the hotel, heard the mingling of music and laughter in the air. Could he go back? Would he want to if he could? He hadn't even thought of that. He'd just thought of getting the annulment finalized and going off to find sanity away from here. To get on with his life.

But now, several questions nudged at him. What if he didn't? What if there wasn't any sanity out there? What if he walked away and Karl was right, he'd regret it for the rest of his life?

"One small piece of advice, if you will," Karl said, cutting into J.T.'s thoughts as they started back toward the hotel.

"Could I stop you?" he asked dryly.

"Indulge me."

"Go ahead."

"Remember, it is so very human to walk away, to give up if things get too complicated or too hard to deal with. Or if one feels hurt or angry. Very human, but the cost can be staggering."

J.T. stopped and looked directly at Karl. "What is this conversation all about?"

"Just conversation over a good cigar." Karl pressed his half-smoked cigar into an ashtray by the door, then turned to J.T. with a look that was oddly somber. "And I thank you for it."

J.T. didn't understand any of this. The whole evening had been that way, jumping from one unreality to another, and nothing was making sense to him. He stubbed out his own cigar next to Karl's, then said, "Thank you."

The older man nodded in a curiously formal way, then said, "The lovely lady you came with has been looking all over for you," just before he stepped inside.

J.T. followed to find the party still going strong, with Vonya in the center of a circle of people, obviously holding court. If she'd been looking for him, she'd given it up in exchange for all the attention from about a dozen people, mostly men.

He glanced away, and that's when he saw Candice. Actually, Candice and Mark dancing to a slow ballad, so close to each other that, as his father used to say, "There ain't no daylight to be seen between 'em." He watched the two of them, and all he could think of was, *She's my wife.* Damn it, that ate at him, and it shouldn't have. Not any more than that perverse jealousy he felt every time he saw Mark touch her.

He needed to sign those annulment papers as soon as he could. He'd get Davis up tonight to start on the paperwork, if he had to, anything to get it over and done with.

"Hey, cowboy, where've you been?" Vonya purred in his ear.

"Getting some air," he said, vaguely annoyed by

the way she was wrapping herself around him as he turned toward her.

"Hey, what's going on?" she asked, drawing back a bit, her dark eyes meeting his.

"Sorry. I've got a lot on my mind."

She slapped him playfully on the arm. "Hey, chill out, and forget about work." She came closer, pressing against him. "Do you want me to get your mind off work?"

Her offer that should have pleased him—and might have at some other time and in some other place—only intensified his annoyance with her. And it wasn't fair to her. He knew that, so he tried to temper his response. "I appreciate the offer, but not right now."

She pouted prettily. "All work and no fun makes cowboys boring."

He couldn't stop looking over at Candice again, then wished he hadn't. Her head was on Mark's shoulder, her eyes closed, and Mark was slowly tracing circles on her back.

"Hey," Vonya was saying, cutting into his thoughts. "What's going on?"

He closed his eyes momentarily, then looked at Vonya. "Nothing. Why?"

"You've changed since we've been here." She looked at a diamond-studded watch she wore on her wrist. "All of six hours." Her dark eyes were on him. "What gives?"

"Hey, J.T.," Jack called to him. "Get on over here."

He turned from Vonya's quizzical look and saw Jack on a raised section near the head table, waving to him with something in his hand. It took him a moment to realize it was the garter. A group of men were in front of Jack, but he was pointing to J.T. "Come on," he called out. "You're holding up the works."

J.T. shook his head, staying where he was. "Oh, go on," Vonya whispered in his ear. "A cowboy with a garter, now that has possibilities."

"Forget that," he said, but she was giggling.

"You're in shape. You can beat all of those wimps, especially those upper-crust yuppies."

J.T. looked at the gathering of men, taken aback to see Mark approaching the group. He would have thought the man would be far too conservative to take part in the tradition. An upper-crust yuppie. He almost smiled, but stopped when he saw Candice a few steps behind Mark, smiling and clapping with the others when Jack started to spin the garter over his head on his forefinger.

"Get on over here, J.T.," Jack was calling again over the din of laughter and clapping.

Candice darted a look in J.T.'s direction, then she turned away as quickly as she'd looked at him. But he didn't miss the way her smile died, or the way she moved farther away from him on the other side of the crowd.

He felt Vonya pushing him softly with her hand at the small of his back. "Go on, go for it," she said, and he moved away from her, toward the group, crossing to where Patrick stood. The little boy, who had taken off his jacket and shirt, but left on his bow tie and vest, was so excited that he was bouncing up and down.

J.T. touched him on the head and he looked up with a brilliant smile. "Way cool, huh, Uncle J.T.?"

"Awesome," J.T. said. "And it's all your doing."

That made the boy's smile grow even more. "Yeah, it's so cool about Sandi and my dad."

J.T. looked up at Jack as his friend shouted, "Good luck, men," and spun the garter off his finger, sending it sailing into the air right at J.T.

Quickly, J.T. lifted Patrick, whispered in his ear, "It's all yours, buddy," and boosted the five-year-old into the air. In a flash, Patrick stretched his hands high above him, and amazingly, managed to grasp the garter with one small hand. J.T. slid him down to the ground and let him go. As the guests cheered, Patrick spun around, holding the garter in the air, then did a victory dance like a football player after making a touchdown.

"I did it! Now what do I win?" he asked J.T.

"You don't exactly win, buddy, but the thinking is that the one who catches the garter is going to be the next guy to get married."

"Married?" Patrick looked horrified, then shook his head emphatically. "No way. Ugh!"

J.T. crouched in front of Patrick. "Surely you know some pretty little girl?"

"I'm only a kid." Patrick looked down at the garter, then held it out to J.T. "Here, you have it. You get married. You're old enough. You can marry that lady you came with. My dad says you should be married and have a bunch of kids to run all over that ranch you have."

J.T. had never thought about kids. He liked them, but on a limited basis. One thing he knew for sure, kids were forever. He'd seen Jack with Patrick, struggling to be a good dad on his own. The commitment was staggering. Children didn't just come into your life, then go out.

He looked over Patrick's head and spotted Candice walking toward Mark. He knew right then that if they'd managed to make a marriage out of what they'd had eight years ago, there would have been children. But nothing about their marriage had been forever.

He looked away from Candice and back down at Patrick. Jack had forever in Patrick, and now in Sandi. He wasn't a man given to envy, but right then, he envied Jack with a vengeance.

CANDICE KEPT HER eyes on Mark as she walked toward him. She never looked in J.T.'s direction, but concentrated on the man in front of her. "Better luck next time," she said to Mark.

He tapped her chin with one finger. "I didn't need any garter to know we're getting married." He gave her a quick kiss on the cheek, then stood back when a soft ringing sound came from his jacket pocket. He took out his cell phone, flipped it open and said, "What is it now?" He listened, then spoke to Candice. "Sorry, it's Taggert. I need to take this call, but it's too noisy out here to hear what he's saying. I won't be a minute."

She wanted to tell him to hang up, to just be here with her and not leave her alone to talk business. But she didn't do anything that silly. Instead, she said, "Go ahead. I'll be fine." She looked past Mark and spotted her mother alone at her table. "I'll go and talk to Mother."

"Good, good," he said, then pressed the phone

to his ear and walked away from her in the direction of the doors into the hotel.

Candice started across to her mother's table, but was startled by squeals of laughter and stopped to look in the direction of the sounds. J.T. and Patrick were tussling, and the little boy was laughing hysterically. The image of J.T. with the little boy in his arms was jarring and, in some way, disturbing.

She'd never thought of J.T. with kids, but it looked right and natural. J.T. as a father, a thought that came from nowhere, but seemed so logical. He'd take his son to the stables on their ranch and let him ride on Joker's back. The huge black horse, who used to be J.T.'s dad's horse, would see a third generation of Watsons. A third generation of hazel-eyed men who could shake the world with a look.

Vonya was there, laughing with J.T. and Patrick. Candice turned from the sight. Some woman would share all of that with J.T., and for one shining moment, she'd thought she'd be that woman, that she'd be the one to bear their children, to watch J.T. show them the ranch, to watch them grow, and she'd be the one to grow old with J.T.

Foolish, stupid ideas, the kind she'd had when she'd thought there could have been love, the kind of love that could be used to build a whole lifetime on. Very stupid, she thought as she headed across to where her mother was sitting.

Eight years. She'd been married for eight years. God, it still rocked her just to think about it. And she had to do more than think about it. She had to make sure the annulment was taken care of this time. No more chances. No more believing that J.T. would take care of it. And she'd do it as soon as she could, put an end to this nightmare.

She watched her mother as she got closer. Grace was at the table by herself, sipping a drink, and the thought of telling her the truth, then asking her what to do, was there. Trying to keep up the facade of being happy, or enjoying this wedding, and saying the right things to Mark, was wearing on her.

The thought came in a rush, but it was killed as quickly as it came when Grace looked up at her as she got close. She smiled slightly, that sort of smile that didn't quite reach her pale blue eyes, then her gaze flicked over Candice. "I saw that you'd changed," she said as Candice reached the table. "My goodness, that other dress..." She feigned a slight shiver. "Well, Sandi really did go all out for this, didn't she?"

She could see her own reaction to the dress in her mother, but now it seemed distasteful to her. Any ideas of talking to her about J.T. were gone. If Grace couldn't get past a dress, how would she get past her daughter being engaged to Mark Forester while still being married to J. T. Watson, a man her parents had never pretended to think was equal to her in any way?

If she could have turned and left, she would have. But she couldn't. "Sandi liked it," she said.

Grace motioned her to the other chair with a flick of her hand. "Don't hover, Candice. Sit down."

Candice took the chair opposite her mother, and spread her hands flat on the cool glass top. She looked at Grace and spoke a thought out loud. "I wish Whitney could have made it back for the wedding."

"I got a call from Dylan just before I left the house, and it looks as if they can make it out on an early flight tomorrow if the weather keeps improving."

Whitney would be home tomorrow. Whitney, the only one who knew about her and J.T. It would be a relief to talk to her. "I'll be glad to have the two of them back."

"So will I." Grace studied her daughter. "Candice, I have the oddest feeling that there's something wrong here."

There was nothing wrong, other than the fact that she'd agreed to marry one man, but was actually married to another. Candice would have laughed at the absurdity of the whole situation, if it hadn't made her want to scream. "What could be wrong?"

Grace fingered her glass, but didn't take a drink. "You tell me."

The opening was there, the perfect prompt to tell her mother everything. But she never got a chance to say anything, because J.T. was suddenly there, his hazel eyes barely flicking to her before turning on her mother.

Chapter Nine

"Ma'am, I'm sorry to interrupt," J.T. drawled, not looking at Candice at all.

She'd forgotten how he'd tried to charm her mother before, and how it had failed. The way it had again. There was no easy smile for J.T., but Grace put on her "polite" face, that partial smile, the direct look, her barrier up.

"Mr. Watson," she said stiffly.

Candice felt her hands pressing so hard on the glass tabletop, she was surprised it didn't crack when J.T. smiled at her mother, oblivious to the slight snub. Or maybe he just didn't care. That would be more his style. "I was wondering if you'd heard anything about Dylan."

"Oh, yes, my son and his bride should be home tomorrow sometime. The weather seems to be clearing."

"That's a relief."

"He'll be pleased to see you, since you didn't make it to his wedding. I know he was very disappointed."

A rebuke at his absence, no matter how mannerly or measured, but now she knew J.T. was ignoring her mother's jabs. He obviously didn't seem to care enough to feel slighted or to have a need to defend himself. "Yes, ma'am," he said. "When you see Dylan, can you tell him I'll try to get in touch with him soon?"

Vonya was there, coming up behind J.T. and looping her hand in his arm. She smiled at the two women. "Hi, there," she said. "Wonderful wedding, isn't it?"

Candice couldn't say a thing, her throat was tightening just watching Vonya pressing close to J.T. and all but rubbing her cheek on his shoulder. But, as usual, Grace did the proper thing. "It's quite unique," she said.

"I'm Vonya," the model said.

"Yes," was all Grace said before looking back at J.T. "Mr. Watson, surely you can tell Dylan that yourself tomorrow when he comes back?"

"I would, but I'm going back to London in a few hours."

"J.T.'s off again," Vonya said, playfully slapping him lightly on the chest. "The man just never lights in one place for very long."

"If y'all would be kind enough to give him my message?" J.T. said.

"Of course." Grace glanced from J.T. to Vonya. "Now, if you'll excuse us?"

J.T. glanced at Candice, the flash from the hazel eyes showing how very wrong she'd been. He wasn't indifferent to the way her mother was treating him or the fact that she'd just dismissed the two of them. There was a flash of real anger there, but he never let it go any further. And in some way that made her feel oddly ashamed of her mother's treatment of them.

He inclined his head and said, ''Of course. We need to be going.''

''Have a good trip,'' Grace said, then turned ever so slightly, using her shoulder to effectively cut off any connection between them and herself and Candice. J.T. walked away with Vonya and Candice couldn't even look at him. She felt ashamed of her mother at that moment, something she'd never felt before in her life.

''Mother, that was rude,'' she said, an understatement, but the only word she could think of besides *cruel.* And her mother wasn't cruel. She was just the product of her life.

Grace looked genuinely taken aback. ''Rude? What are you talking about?''

She bit her lip. ''J.T. is Dylan's friend.''

Grace shrugged. ''Of course he is, dear, but then again, I never understood what he and Dylan had in common. The man would rather ride a horse than ride in a car. He even changed into jeans and boots. Can you believe that, at a wedding? And he brought that model person. One name, really.'' She shook her head. ''And he has that way of calling everyone 'darlin'.'''

Candice remembered the first time J.T. had called her darlin'. She shivered slightly, and closed her eyes momentarily before looking back at her mother. ''He's just not up to Montgomery standards, even with all his money, is he?''

Grace shrugged slightly and glanced past Candice. ''Do you remember that year before you went off to college and Dylan graduated?''

She clasped her hands together tightly on the glass tabletop, never taking her eyes off her mother. "Of course I do."

"John was obviously wrong, but he kept telling me that he was sure you had a crush on J.T." She grimaced. "It almost drove him crazy. He talked about telling J.T. that he had to leave, or sending you away on a world tour or something. But all of that doesn't matter now, because J.T. did leave, and he never came back." She chuckled softly. "And you got to Europe anyway."

Candice felt real anger in her, mostly aimed at her father, but some was reserved for her mother. Yet, wasn't that exactly the reaction she'd known they both would have had? Wasn't that why she'd tried to pull back from J.T., to regain sanity, to figure out how to approach her family? The very reason J.T. had walked away. He'd said he wouldn't wait around for her to grow up and away from her parents' control. And he hadn't.

But to hear her mother tell her that her father knew what was going on, that he could tell she was falling head over heels for J.T.? That stunned her. She'd thought she was so controlled, so subtle. She would have laughed if she didn't feel so sick about everything.

"He hated J.T. that much?"

"Oh, no, not at all. He rather liked him, actually, but he wasn't the man your father envisioned for you." She fingered her half-empty goblet. "I always thought he was a nice young man, too. Oh, a bit rough around the edges, but he was actually a pretty good friend to Dylan and he had manners."

''Just not the proper lineage?'' she asked, her tone flat in her own ears.

''Oh, dear, that sounds so...so...''

''Snobby, class-conscious?'' she supplied tightly.

Her mother looked as if that assessment had flustered her, not an easy thing to do to Grace Montgomery. ''Candice, that's enough.'' She waved it aside with one small hand. ''Besides, it doesn't matter. John and I were wrong, and you're engaged to a man who is everything you could want. This talk is just silly.''

Silly wasn't the word she'd use. She had to swallow twice before she could talk again. ''What if...what if you'd been right, if Father had been right?''

Grace actually laughed at that, a brittle sound. ''Candice, we weren't, and now you're getting married to Mark. I'd say that all's well that ends well, wouldn't you?'' She motioned past Candice. ''And it looks as if Mr. Watson is doing quite well. Dylan tells me his businesses flourish, and he certainly isn't short on women.''

Candice turned and J.T. was dancing with Vonya. Her heart literally hurt when he laughed and swept Vonya into a twirl. He looked as if he didn't have a care in the world. Nothing was bothering him. She turned back to her mother. ''Yes, everything's just fine.''

''Where's Mark?''

''Taking a business call.''

Grace glanced down at her drink. ''You know, he reminds me very much of John when we first met.''

Mark seemed nothing like her father, beyond being so work involved and from a family that could trace its roots back to the founding fathers. "Really? How?"

Grace looked at Candice, her eyes strangely bright. "He's very attractive, very attentive, from a good family, and he's a man who goes after what he wants." She looked down at her drink again as she said softly, "As I said, very much like John."

Candice had never thought much about her parents' relationship, beyond the fact that they seemed distant from each other for most of her life. Even when her father had died, she never saw her mother cry. She narrowed her eyes. Was that what she was seeing? Her mother on the verge of tears? If she was, she knew Grace wouldn't cry, not here and not now, if ever.

"Are you all right, Mother?" she asked.

Grace looked up at Candice, her eyes overly bright, but with no trace of dampness. "Of course I'm fine." She glanced at the party. "I shouldn't have come, that's all. I wasn't going to, but I felt it would have been rude not to make an appearance."

Always the one to do "the right thing" for appearances. But no joy in doing it. "It's a nice gesture." That sounded stilted, but Candice didn't know what else to say.

Grace took a genteel sip of her drink, then carefully put the goblet back on the table. "The proper thing to do, don't you think?" she asked.

Candice had felt edgy enough with her own circumstances, but seeing this side of her mother, a side fighting to contain her emotions, yet seeming so very vulnerable, was unnerving. "Mother, what's wrong?"

Grace sat back, absentmindedly fingering the goblet. She sighed, a soft sound that Candice could barely hear over the music and noises of the party. "Nothing," she finally said. "Nothing at all. What on earth could be wrong? Dylan is happy and you've got Mark. Life is very right at the moment." She smiled slightly, a knowing smile that Candice had seen before. "Before Mark asked you to marry him, did you know he asked me if he could?"

She knew her mouth must have dropped. "He what?"

"I'm your parent."

"I can't believe he'd do that," she said softly.

"He was being very thoughtful, Candice," she said with a touch of exasperation.

He did "the right thing," and that pleased her mother. It would have pleased her father, too. "I guess you told him he could have me?"

She shrugged, a fluttery motion of tiny shoulders. "I told him John would approve, and that I approved. But it was up to you."

"Thanks."

Grace took another drink. "You know, John chose Mark for you years ago. He wouldn't have tolerated anyone else."

Candice could feel her chest tighten. "Tolerate? What are you talking about?"

"Oh, he knew you'd do the right thing. That you would make the right choice."

She felt cold all over. "Did he?"

"Yes, and you and Mark will have a wonderful wedding that will go smoothly, unlike your brother's wedding. And you'll have the life I always dreamed you would have."

That brought back a chunk of reality with a painful thud. She couldn't marry Mark until she got the annulment. "Mother, do you know if Ron Buchanan can take care of family matters?"

"Ron? He's a corporate lawyer, but I'm sure..." She paused, then nodded as if she understood something. "Oh, of course. A prenuptial agreement. A wonderful idea to protect everything, although with Mark, I don't believe you'd need it. But, better to do it and not live to regret not having done it later on."

It always came back to money and the family. Always. But she'd never even thought about a prenuptial. "Do you know if Ron is in San Francisco, or is he back in New York?"

"I wouldn't know, but Dylan would. Since he and Ron are so close, he'd know for sure."

She hadn't thought of that. Dylan and Ron were close. The last thing she wanted was a friend of Dylan's knowing about the annulment. There had to be someone else to contact. "I guess he would."

"You can at least ask Ron who is the best at prenups."

"Sure, I can ask him that," she replied and suddenly remembered that J.T. had said he was leaving for London almost immediately. Panic grew in her. If he left without taking care of the annulment, she'd be back to square one. Still married to him and engaged to Mark. The panic seemed to choke her and she stood. "Excuse me, Mother," she said in a rush. "I need to talk to someone."

She didn't wait for her mother to respond before turning and leaving the table. She had to talk to J.T. again and make very sure they were going to get the annulment as quickly and as quietly as possible.

But when she spotted him, he was with Jack by the bar. The two men were deep in conversation. She hesitated, then saw Mark and, instead of going over to him as he stepped out onto the terrace, she turned and slipped through a side door and out of sight.

She didn't want to talk to Mark right now, not when she could feel her heart racing, and she knew she would be unable to keep up a semblance of polite conversation. She had to talk to J.T. first. But she had to wait until he was alone.

"I THREW THAT GARTER to you, buddy," Jack said as the waiter handed both men their drinks. "But you ducked it."

"Exactly," J.T. said, taking a sip of his drink.

"And where's the tux?" Jack asked.

"Right next to yours," J.T. said, moving toward the railing of the terrace.

As he turned to Jack, he caught a glimpse of Candice walking quickly across the terrace and through a side door. The simple dress she was wearing was even more provocative for what it didn't show than the ruined dress had been for what it did show. Then she disappeared inside, and he exhaled a breath he hadn't even been aware he'd been holding until then.

"Hey, J.T.?" Jack said, turning to look in the direction of his gaze, then back to him. "I think you lied to me, buddy."

"What are you babbling about? What lie did I tell you now?"

"That you and Candice are nothing to each other. I think you said, you're over and done, that she's got her...what was it? Oh, yes, overgrown yuppie that good old dad approved of.''

"Jack, don't go down that road," J.T. said tightly. "Not if you know what's good for you."

"Or what? You'll rope and tie me?" He grinned to take the edge off both of their words. "Hey, if I can't call you on this, who can?"

"Who says I need to be called on it?"

"If that look you gave her as she left is any hint of what's going on in that mind and libido of yours, I'd say you're still tied up in knots over her, annulment or not."

The waiter was there with the drinks and both men took one. While Jack sipped his, J.T. tossed half of his down in one gulp. Then he looked right at Jack. "There is no annulment. There never was."

Jack's mouth almost dropped to the floor. "What in the hell?"

"I thought she got it. She thought I got it. Never did, neither one of us. Major, huge foul-up, and we didn't even know until tonight."

Jack looked genuinely confused. "You're trying to tell me—"

"That we're still married."

Jack shook his head. "Okay, now what?"

"We finish what we started," J.T. said. "She's getting her attorney on it first thing Monday."

"I can't believe that you've been married eight years and you never knew. What if one of you'd gotten married? Good God, you'd be a bigamist."

He'd never come close, not after Candice. "She's getting married," he muttered. "That's why she wants this taken care of quietly. Mr. Old-Money Yuppie doesn't know a thing about it."

"Neither does her mother, does she?"

"No." He didn't want to think about Grace Montgomery and that little show she'd put on in front of Vonya. He was still seething about that. "As far as I know, you're the only one besides her and me. A skeleton in the proverbial closet of the Montgomery family. And a skeleton Candice wants buried quickly and quietly."

"How about you?"

J.T. exhaled. "I'll get Davis on it as soon as I can call him."

"Are you sure?"

"Sure about what?" he asked, putting his glass down on a side table.

"Letting it go."

J.T. turned from Jack and looked out over the ocean. He gripped the wall with both hands and stared out into the night.

"Well?" Jack said from beside him.

"It never existed," J.T. said. "So, there's nothing to let go of."

"So you say."

J.T. turned to Jack, anger starting to build in him. "What does that mean?"

"I saw the way you looked at her. How you acted when she was with Mark. There's nothing at all there?"

"She's getting married, Jack, and that's that. The end. Finito, done, finished. There's nothing to do."

He glanced away and spotted Grace Montgomery sitting alone at a table. She sat with her back to the view, cradling a goblet in her hands. "And her mother's going to be thrilled. The perfect man for her perfect daughter." He sucked in air. "I think

Candice was absolutely right to walk away after that fiasco. Can you imagine what her parents would have put her through if she'd produced me as a husband?''

''Hell,'' Jack said simply as he followed J.T.'s gaze. ''Her mother's a beautiful woman, isn't she, even at her age.''

He'd always thought she was an incredibly lovely woman who had given her daughter all that beauty in a more spectacular package. The way she gave her daughter her sense of place, a daughter who chose to fit in perfectly. She'd schooled her children in their position in society. Dylan loved his mother and had almost made a disastrous marriage for the business's sake. Now Candice...

She's done her job well, he thought as he watched Grace brush at her perfectly styled hair with elegant fingers. ''Does she still play the piano, those sonatas at the huge black grand piano in their music room?''

''Sandi mentioned that when she'd visit Candice, Grace would play for hours.''

He watched her exhale, then close her eyes momentarily. A delicate-looking person, yet a person strong enough to put you in your place with a single look or a flick of her tiny hand. ''Did she take her husband's death hard?''

''From what I was told, she's basically put in almost a full year of mourning for the man.''

He never would have thought there was enough love in that marriage for her to put her life on hold for that long. But, then again, that was the socially correct thing to do. And Grace Montgomery always did the socially correct thing. Just the way her daughter did. He glanced away and saw Mark approaching Grace's table. Just the sight of the man made his stomach knot.

"Did you hear how Candice took her father's death?" J.T. asked.

"Dylan said she took it like a Montgomery."

Like a Montgomery who wouldn't cry or needed to be held far into the night.

"Too bad," he muttered, then saw Sandi coming toward them. "And here comes the bride."

"Sounds like a song to me," Jack said. "We're going to make our escape. Her sister's going to take care of Patrick for a while. How about you? Are you going to stay for a while, or are you jetting off somewhere tonight?"

"London. I've got unfinished business there."

"Too bad you can't wait to see Dylan when he gets here."

"Can't this time. I'll meet up with him in San Francisco later on."

"Call me when you are and I'll try to get up there, too."

"You got a deal."

"And, J.T.?"

"What?"

He hesitated, then shook his head. "What are you going to do?"

"Take care of things," he said.

"Well, good luck," Jack said.

J.T. held out his hand, and when Jack took it in his, J.T. pulled him to him in a bear hug. "Thanks and good luck to you, too," he said as they stood back. "Now go and have a hell of a honeymoon."

"That's the plan," Jack said and headed over to Sandi.

J.T. stayed by the terrace wall while Jack and Sandi left in a shower of confetti, rice and well wishes from the guests. He turned away as they disappeared through the open doors into the hotel. He saw Grace Montgomery stand. She glanced in his direction, inclined her head slightly, then turned and walked quietly away.

J.T. was ready to leave, too, to get the hell out of town. He had no reason to be here any longer. He looked around for Vonya, but couldn't see her anywhere. So he crossed to the doors where Sandi and Jack had exited and went inside, heading for the elevators.

He checked his watch as he strode across the lobby area. He'd call Davis, catch the red-eye and get to London in just enough time to go over the details before the meetings started tomorrow.

As he got into the elevator, he fought the memory of Candice in the elevator with him earlier. *"Sometimes we just have to walk away and let things go,"* he'd told Karl, and that's what he was going to do.

But Karl's questions haunted him. *"No regrets? Just leave?"*

He hit the button for his floor and leaned back against the coolness of the mirrors. *"Remember, it is so very human to walk away...very human, but the cost can be staggering."* Even with the man not there, Karl kept nudging at him.

He pushed himself up straight as the elevator stopped, and he stepped out into the corridor. As he walked down to his room, he tried to shut out the older man's words, but they wouldn't die. Regrets? Hell, sure he regretted what had happened. Who wouldn't regret the impetuousness of eloping and finding out it was a huge mistake? That his new wife cared more about what her family thought than about being with him?

God, that sounded like self-pity and he wasn't into that. He unlocked his door and slipped inside, but the first thing he saw when he turned on a light was a pair of women's shoes on the floor by the door. And they weren't Vonya's. They were traces of Candice. The same traces that tangled in his mind and wouldn't let go of her scent and the way she felt under him.

He walked past the shoes, leaving them where they were, and crossed to the phone on a side table near the bed. The mussed bed. Mussed because of his time here with Candice. The taste of her was surely still in his mouth, the way the feel of her was imprinted on his skin.

He turned his back on the sight and with a muttered oath punched in the numbers for his assistant's home. When Davis finally answered, he could tell the man had been asleep, but once he heard J.T.'s voice, he cleared his throat. "There isn't anything from London and I don't think that—"

"Just listen to me," J.T. said, cutting him off. "I need you to get right on something for me."

"Of course. What?"

"An annulment."

"I'm sorry, for a minute I thought you said…an annulment. Our connection must be bad."

"It's fine. I said annulment. Find out what's involved in getting one as quickly and as quietly as possible."

"What state are we talking about?"

"California, but the marriage was in Nevada."

The man never asked for any further clarification, just agreed to do it right away, then said, "And London?"

"I'll make the flight out of San Francisco." He suddenly felt tired, almost soul-weary. "I'll meet you there."

"Okay. Sir, what do you want me to do with the annulment information?"

"Bring it with you," he said and hung up.

He laid the receiver back in the cradle, then stripped off his shirt and sat on the bed to tug off his boots and socks. Eight years. He still couldn't believe it. He dropped his boots and socks onto the carpet. Damn it, he never knew. All this time. Married.

A truth suddenly came to him, sliding into his thoughts before he could block it. He still wanted her. Every atom of his being responded to her. Despite the fact that she was engaged to another man. Despite the fact that the "Montgomery" wall was still built around her, he'd never stopped wanting her.

He could almost feel the ache in his body from those moments when she'd been on this bed with him, when he'd touched her and kissed her. And it overlapped with the need that had been in him eight years ago. Wanting her was one thing. Having her was another completely. Nothing had changed. Nothing. Not even that she wanted out of their marriage.

There was a soft knock on the door, and he pulled himself out of the darkness of those thoughts. Vonya was back to get changed for her flight to Saint Tropez. Thank goodness she was leaving soon. The last thing he wanted was any complications with her to-night.

He headed across the room, reached the door and pulled it open. But Vonya wasn't there. Instead, he was faced with his past and his present...Candice.

Chapter Ten

Candice knew she shouldn't have come up to J.T.'s room, but she hadn't had a choice. When he'd disappeared, she'd felt panicked. He was going to London and she had the horrible feeling that once he was gone, the annulment would never be resolved. They'd be tied up in a sham marriage forever. And that scared her.

She'd come up to see if he was still here, but she hadn't expected him to answer the door half-dressed. Just jeans. That was all. She felt her mouth go dry at the sight of his bare chest, the pattern of hair forming a T on his tanned skin, and his stomach... She had to swallow hard to be able to get out words.

"I'm glad you're still here," she said quickly.

That made a smile flick at the corners of his mouth, and that only made her throat tighten more. "I'm still here," he said.

Then she realized he was half dressed, and he was sharing the room with Vonya. She ignored the slight sickness that thought produced and tried to look past J.T. into the room. But he moved to block her view, and she had the distinct feeling he knew what she was doing. "Can you talk?" she asked, giving up.

''Darlin', I've been talking nonstop since I was two years old.''

''J.T., I meant...'' She couldn't stand that teasing smile. ''Are you alone?''

''Yes, I'm alone, darlin',' he said. ''Vonya's off somewhere enjoying the party.''

There was a dinging sound at the elevators that startled Candice, and she darted a look down the hall. As if talking about her made her materialize, Vonya was there, stepping off the elevator. If the tall woman felt any surprise or jealousy seeing Candice there, she didn't show it. She just smiled as she came closer, ''Hey you two, no fair having a party and not inviting me.''

Candice hadn't wanted anyone to see her up here, especially Vonya. Now the woman was here, heading right for J.T. With aching familiarity, Vonya wrapped her arms around his neck and smiled at him. ''No fair, cowboy.'' She pressed a hand to his bare chest over his heart. ''You know how much I love a good party.''

''We were just talking,'' J.T. said.

Vonya looked at Candice. ''Oh sure, of course. I know what this is all about,'' she said.

Candice felt her heart lurch. She knew.

''You know what?'' J.T. asked.

The apprehension eased a bit as the woman said, ''You two were talking about Dylan, right?''

''What about him?'' J.T. asked.

''They were just saying that he and Whitney called and they're going to fly out tonight, instead of tomorrow. The weather's cleared, so they're getting out of there earlier than they thought.''

Candice was almost light-headed with relief.

"That's great," she managed to say around the tightness in her throat.

"Sure is. I wish I could meet the guy. I've heard so much about him." Vonya looked at J.T. "Too bad we have to get going, sweetie, but the shuttle's flying out in an hour or so."

That panic was back. He was just going to fly off and leave this all unresolved. "J.T.," Candice said quickly. "We have to...to talk."

"Sweetie, we need to go now," Vonya was saying as her hands lowered to grasp his upper arm. "We've got a ride offer." She looked at Candice. "That nice Mr. Delaney had a limo on standby, but he says he doesn't need it, so he's offered it to us to get to the airport." She looked back at J.T. "So, hurry up and get dressed. It's downstairs right now with the engine running. Grab your stuff." She grinned. "And add some clothes, okay?"

Candice all but held her breath, knowing she couldn't say anything else, but willing J.T. to at least give her a few more minutes. He'd never done what Candice had wanted him to do before, and she didn't have any reason to think he'd start now, but amazingly he did. "I can't leave just yet," he said.

"Sweetie, of course you can. Just throw on a shirt, get your boots and hat and we're out of here." She was actually tugging at him now. "We'll make our connecting flights easily if we go now."

He looked from Vonya to Candice, then he said, "Wait right here." With that, he turned to Vonya and went into the room with the woman. The door swung partially closed, staying open an inch or so. Just enough for Candice to hear the voices inside.

"I can't leave right now," J.T. was saying. "There's a problem I need to take care of."

"Here?" Vonya asked, her voice a bit farther away, as if she was moving around the room as she spoke.

"Problems follow me around," he said.

Now Vonya was closer and her voice lowered seductively. "Oh, come on. You've got your cell phone, and you can take care of any problem while we drive. Besides, we'll have the limo all to ourselves. That has real possibilities." Then there was silence, prolonged silence, and Candice turned away from the door. "Let me show you what you'll be missing." Candice moved back, leaning against the wall on the far side of the corridor, and closed her eyes. But she opened them immediately when all she could visualize was J.T. and Vonya in the bedroom. That was something she didn't want to imagine. Then J.T. was talking again, his voice lower and rougher.

"Vonya, I know what I'm missing, trust me. Keep that thought, and once London is done, we'll pick up where we left off."

"Okay, cowboy," she breathed huskily, and her tone raised goose bumps on Candice's arms. "If that's a promise..."

"Oh, you bet it is, darlin'," J.T. said heartily.

Candice shivered and the door was moving. She stood straight, bracing herself. Then J.T. was there, and Vonya was coming out carrying a single small bag. She stopped by J.T. and grinned at him as she touched his cheek with the tips of her fingers. "Don't forget," she murmured. She drew back and looked at Candice with a smile. "Men," she said with a shake of her head. "Business, business, business."

Candice knew that her smile was tight, but Vonya didn't seem to notice. She turned back to J.T. "You be good and, if you can't, have fun," she said on a laugh.

"Absolutely," he replied.

Then Vonya was going down the hallway to the elevators. The doors slid open and as she got to them, she looked back. "Later, cowboy," she called, blew him a kiss, then got in the car and the doors closed.

Candice took a breath, trying to find some balance. She felt like a voyeur and the feeling wasn't good at all. Then J.T. was looking at her, and as she really looked at him, she cringed. Lipstick traces were on his lips, and she grabbed at anger to get her through this.

"Wipe your face, J.T., that shade doesn't become you," she said in disgust.

All that did was make him grin before he swiped a hand over his mouth, taking away the traces of lipstick. "They ought to invent lipstick that doesn't do that," he commented. "Better?"

She nodded. "Gone."

"Good. Now we're alone, so what's going on?"

But they weren't alone. The elevator dinged again, and Candice didn't wait to see who was getting off. With her luck it would be Mark. Quickly, she moved past J.T. and into his room. She was making her escape, but the minute she was in the room, she knew she'd have done better staying in the hallway.

She almost tripped over his boots and socks, then

she looked up and saw the bed, still the same as when she'd left earlier. A definite mistake coming in here, she thought, but when she turned to leave, J.T. was there, closing the door and facing her.

The memory of the madness that had happened last time was too fresh in her mind, but she knew that was foolish. Just say what you need to say and get out, she told herself, but turned from the sight of J.T. and stared out the windows at the night. She wished the windows opened so she could breathe fresh air. But she had to settle for watching the full moon, the stars and the peace of the water far below. All of the peace that she'd lost since seeing J.T. again.

"Okay, what's going on?" J.T. repeated from somewhere behind her.

She stared hard at the night outside, wanting to sound calm and controlled, but found she couldn't stop a tightness in her voice. "You said that you were going to London right away when you were downstairs."

"I didn't think you'd heard me," he said. "I'm sure your mother didn't."

"But you're going?" she asked, not wanting to talk about her mother right now, or that encounter downstairs.

"That's right, darlin'. I'm catching the shuttle as soon as we finish here."

She turned, and his eyes were shadowed, but nothing hid the way he had his fingertips tucked into the top of his jean pockets, or the way he was rocking slightly forward on the balls of his feet.

"But you said you'd start the annulment proceedings right away. We can't let the same thing happen that happened last time.''

She hated that edge of panic in her voice, so she took a breath before saying as calmly as possible, ''I mean, you'd think I'm doing something and I'd think you're doing something, and no one's doing anything. Just like last time.''

''That won't happen again,'' he said.

''It can't, J.T.,'' she said quickly. ''This whole thing is so unbelievably messy. I...we can't take that chance.''

He studied her intently, and for no reason she could fathom, he seemed angered by her words. Then he came toward her, slowly, with measured steps. And the panic was building in her as a buffer was being dissolved. ''I guess that's what we did, didn't we?''

She couldn't focus with him this close. ''We did what?''

''We took a chance.''

''And it didn't work, J.T.'' He was closer still, and that closeness was triggering all sorts of unwelcome responses and thoughts, accompanied by an aching need in her middle. ''It has to be over and done, J.T.''

''Then we'll take care of it.''

''But you're going to London.''

''I'm not going to fall off the face of the earth,'' he said softly, but that's just what it felt as if he'd done last time. Walked away and disappeared for eight years. ''Davis always knows exactly where I am. The man is amazing, better than radar at tracking me down.'' He rocked toward her, his voice even lower. "Don't worry. This time we'll do it right."

"Right?" she breathed, unnerved that her eyes were damp. She couldn't be close to tears. There was no reason for tears. All he'd said was they hadn't done it right the first time. Not even close. But she remembered how right it had felt, at least for a few moments in time. "Sure, we...we will."

A tear slipped down her cheek, but before she could swipe it away, J.T. was there, brushing at it with the tip of his finger. "Now that's a very un-Montgomery-like thing to do," he whispered.

Damn the Montgomery thing, she thought, but just sniffled. "I'm...I'm just tired and this has been such a shock."

"Damn it, darlin', don't do this to me."

She shook slightly at his touch. "D-don't do this to me," she managed to say in a choking voice.

"Do what?" he whispered. "This?" He traced his finger along her jawline to her chin. "Or this?" His finger tipped her chin up, and she was looking up at him. "Don't say I'm sorry for this whole mess?"

It hadn't all been a mess. Not all of it. But no words came to her as more tears slipped down her cheeks.

"Darlin', don't," he said softly, but she couldn't stop it. Not even when his thumb made a slow circle on her skin.

"J.T., I just need this done." Please let it end. "I need..."

He shifted his hand to her throat and her words died out as he gently cupped the nape of her neck under her hair. With exquisite slowness, he drew her closer to him, and there was nothing in her right then to fight the inevitable. She was against him, letting him hold her, and it felt right. The support, the holding. Not being alone.

She realized then that she'd felt alone for so long she couldn't remember when she'd felt connected. No, that wasn't true. She knew the last time she'd felt connected. It had been with J.T. The very last time. When they'd been younger and crazy and in love. That last thought wrenched her to her soul and she pushed it back. Why did she always try to label what happened between them as love? It hadn't been. But even as she thought it, she knew that was a lie. At least for her.

She drew back, looking up at J.T., and a realization came without any warning. She'd really loved him back then. She moved back farther, thankful for the cool air against her skin instead of his touch. She'd never known until now that she'd really loved him. She swiped at the dampness on her cheeks, and felt her heart sink. She'd let it all go.

"Oh, God," she breathed more to herself than to J.T. "I'm sorry." Very sorry that it had been over before she'd even known it had begun. And now there was no going back. "This has been a terrible day."

J.T. looked down at her, at the delicate loveliness about her, and the incredible sadness in her. And all he wanted to do right then was to make her smile, to take away the misery he could see there. The one way he knew to do that was to make things right with her about the annulment, then she could get on with her life with Mark. That last part was jarring, but true.

"Okay, just tell me what attorney you're dealing with and I'll take care of everything."

She shrugged, a fluttery, painful, vulnerable motion. Almost as disturbing as right then when she wiped her hand over her mouth before speaking. "I was going to use the company attorney, but he's so close to Dylan. I..." She shrugged again, a sharper motion this time. "I'll have to find someone tomorrow. As soon as I can."

"I've got an idea."

She stared at him, her lashes still damp. "What?"

"There isn't anything at stake here—no money, no holdings, no prenuptial agreement. It's a simple dissolution, just the way it would have been before. A simple mistake. Would you have any problem with my attorney just taking care of the whole thing, both sides?"

A simple mistake? A simple mistake that had all but torn her heart out. "I...I guess that would be okay," she managed to say.

He faced something then, something simple and clear that he'd known all along. She wanted this over and done. And no matter how much he recognized the fact that they still had a physical need for each other, in every other way, she didn't need him. She didn't want him in her life.

"Let me make a call and get this going," he said, crossing away from her to the phone by the bed. He reached for it, pushed in numbers, then had Davis on the line. "Get me Jacob, and three-way it. Listen in and take notes."

"But, sir, it's past midnight, well past midnight."

"Just get him."

"Yes, sir, hold on."

The line clicked, then went quiet. J.T. could sense Candice moving behind him, but he didn't turn. "He's getting the attorney on the line."

"Will this take long?" she asked, just wanting to get out of the room and away from J.T. and her own weaknesses.

Shadows touched his throat and eyes. "A few minutes. Why didn't you want to use your attorney?"

"He and Dylan have been good friends for a long time, and I know he isn't supposed to say anything to anyone, you know, attorney-client privilege, but it could slip."

She really didn't want a soul to know about this, especially Mark. "My guy is trustworthy and someone who can keep his mouth shut. No one will ever know about this, not unless you tell them."

"Thanks," she said simply. "We really need to get this worked out."

She nibbled on her bottom lip, and J.T. could almost taste her on his lips. A stupid thing to imagine, but it was almost real to him. When she'd cried, holding her hadn't been the only thing he'd wanted to do for her. Not even close. There was only one thing that had ever worked out between them.

Davis was back on the line. "He's calling you in five minutes. I gave him the number at the hotel. Do you want him on the cell phone? I can call him back."

"No, this is fine. I'll be here." He hung up. "The attorney is calling back in a few minutes, then we'll get this all settled."

He saw her look around, her nervousness obvious. "So, a few minutes?" she said, turning back to the windows, then back to him. "He can do this quietly?"

"I told you he can and he will. God knows he's being paid enough for his discretion." She was fiddling with her hand and he finally realized she was twisting her engagement ring around and around on her finger. "Darlin', take it easy. You're going to wear that ring out before you and Mark even get married."

She stopped, clasping her hands together. "I just want..."

"I know what you want," he said, moving closer, not even thinking about what he really wanted. "And you'll get it." Unlike himself. "I started this, and I'll finish it."

She took a shaky breath, then glanced at him, her eyes shadowed by the low light, but the connection was enough to make his body tighten. "It isn't all your fault," she whispered.

"Okay, we did it together." He could feel her body heat brush his bare chest, and his body tightened even more. "We'll share the responsibility for the mess." He looked down at her and words came that he hadn't intended to say. "But it wasn't all bad, was it?"

Her tongue darted out to touch her lips, and the action unnerved him. "No, it wasn't. Just..."

"Just?" he prodded, so close he could hear her take a breath before speaking.

"Nothing."

"Oh, darlin'," he said, "it definitely wasn't nothing. Not the way I remember it."

She shook her head. "J.T., don't."

Something in him drove him on, words coming

that he knew shouldn't be said, but wouldn't stop. "Don't remind you that there was one thing we did and did damn well? Hell, better than that, I'd have called it spectacular, actually."

She hugged her arms around herself, crushing her breasts, but she couldn't hide the way her breathing was getting more rapid. She remembered. He knew damn well she remembered. It couldn't all be in his head, that single night that had shattered his world. A single night that made the rest of his life look like an afterthought.

He could barely absorb where his thoughts were going, down a road to a conclusion that he knew he'd regret finding. Something snapped in him. He was doomed to remember this woman for the rest of his life, he knew that, but she could and would walk out and forget. She could go out the door into Mark's arms and act as if what they'd had had never been. Anger burned in him, right alongside a need for her that was staggering.

Without any plan, he pulled her to him, up against him, and the world became an overwhelming place of sensations and need. Her body against his, her breath on his skin, then the kiss. It came of its own volition and had a life of its own.

The connection was shattering to J.T., something that he never expected and never experienced before in life. Except once. That night. One night. When he and Candice had made love and he'd known he was the first. The only one. The night he loved her more than life itself.

That thought was as shattering as the kiss. He'd loved her? Was that it? God, he could barely grab at the word, but it fit someway. Had he been lying to everyone and himself? Her hands drew along his bare back and the reality of the contact with her was so intense, he trembled. Love? He could barely comprehend what that could mean, and drew back, looking down into her face, her lips softly parted, her eyes half-closed.

He wasn't sure if it was love, but he knew right then the magnitude of the lies he'd been telling himself for eight years. That she was nothing to him, that he was well rid of her, that he didn't care, that he'd forgotten everything. The truth was, he remembered everything, every touch, every kiss, all the memories had been there, stored away in his soul until now. And the truth in those memories rocked his world.

Right now, she was everything to him. He had regrets about eight long years alone that tore at his heart. He needed her. He wanted her. And he didn't want that damn annulment. He took a shuddering breath as she jerked back from him and out of his reach.

His loss was staggering when her touch on his bare chest was gone and, instinctively, he reached out to her again. But she drew back farther, scrubbing the back of her hand across her lips. Then the phone rang. A shrill summons that cut through whatever was going on between them.

He stared at her as it rang and rang, then flinched when she muttered, ''Answer it.''

He turned and reached for it, pressing it to his ear. ''Yes?''

He heard the attorney talking, asking questions, but J.T. couldn't begin to focus on what the man was saying. Instead, he interrupted him. ''Hold for a minute," he said and pressed the hold button before turning back to Candice. His desire was undiminished, and he knew he needed her out of here if he was going to make sense out of anything. "This is going to take some time."

Candice could feel her heart hammering against her ribs and fire burned within her. She continued to wipe her mouth, to try to obliterate the taste of J.T. lingering there. She'd loved him, but this was a physical thing for him, a basic, physical thing, she reasoned as she tried to catch her breath. He'd just kissed Vonya, probably the same way. No, it didn't mean anything beyond that to him.

She deliberately looked away from those eyes, but she wished she hadn't. His arousal was more than evident, and he wasn't doing a thing to hide it. He didn't care that she saw it, and that only underlined the fact that this was all physical to him. Satisfying desire, not anything deeper than that.

She turned away from him toward the windows, pressing both hands to her middle. Damn him, he tore at her, devastating her, and yet he seemed so controlled now. As if moments ago he hadn't been kissing her as if he could taste her soul. She hated him desperately at that moment.

Chapter Eleven

"How long will it take?" Candice managed to ask, closing her eyes so tightly, colors exploded behind her lids.

"I'm not sure." She sensed J.T. moving behind her, but thank goodness when he spoke again, he wasn't any closer to her. "But it could take a while."

She couldn't just wait here with him. She knew how impossible that would be. She hugged her arms around her middle as she turned, braced to face him again. "I can't just stay here," she said. "I'm expected and—"

"I understand," he said. "Why don't you let me talk to him, then I'll just meet you in the lobby at eight tomorrow morning."

"I thought you were taking off for London?"

"I can put London on hold for a bit to take care of this." He came closer, but thankfully didn't make any attempt to reach out to her again. She wasn't at all sure what would happen if he did. Their physical connection had never been in question. It was everything else about their relationship that had been wrong.

''We'll finish this before I leave. That's my wedding present to you and Forester.'' He rocked forward slightly on the balls of his feet and his voice dropped. ''And the least I can do for my wife.''

That shook her and she muttered, ''Don't say that.''

''I'm trying to help,'' he said softly. ''I'm tired of seeing you so upset.''

She swiped at her face. ''I'm just tired, and this...this is all so...''

''Upsetting?''

''Yes.''

''Disturbing?''

''Yes.''

''Unsettling?''

She clasped her hands tightly in front of her. ''Yes.''

''Troubling?''

She looked at him, and despite everything, she felt a smile twitch at her lips. ''J.T. Enough.''

''Just trying to cover all the territory,'' he said with a half grin.

''You have.'' She moved to go past him, making very sure she didn't touch him again. ''I have to go.''

She quickly crossed the room and headed for the door, but she'd barely touched the knob when his voice stopped her. ''Darlin'?''

He called everyone darlin', but every time he said the word, it did something to her. ''What?'' she asked without turning.

''Don't forget, the lobby at eight.''

She nodded.

''And darlin'?''

She closed her eyes. "What?"

"I just realized something."

"What's that?"

"Tomorrow's our anniversary."

He had to be kidding. She turned, and he hadn't moved from the spot where she'd left him. But even from that distance, she could see he wasn't joking. Then she realized he was right. The date was right. Eight years ago tomorrow they'd eloped. "How…how did you remember?"

"How could I forget?" he replied.

And tomorrow they'd end it all. They would dissolve the marriage as if it had never begun. She trembled and covered her emotion by moving abruptly to turn and grab the doorknob, open it, then leave without looking back.

She stepped into the hall, closed the door behind her and didn't stop walking until she was in the elevator and heading down to the lobby. If she could just get out of here without seeing Mark, she'd be okay. She knew she would be. As long as she didn't have to see him and smile and pretend that everything was wonderful.

An anniversary? She'd never thought of it like that, but J.T. was right. The eight-year mark of the biggest mistake of her life. Yet even as she thought that, she knew it was the eight-year mark of a heady, exciting, passionate twenty-four hours.

She leaned against the back of the elevator and remembered the girl who had gone with J.T. The one who had known she wanted to be with him, the one who had told him there hadn't been any other man in her life. The one who had said it was marriage or nothing. And he hadn't missed a beat.

"*Well, darlin',*" he'd said in that drawl. "*Marriage it is.*"

She couldn't even blame it on the drinks, or the night or madness. It was pure need and wanting, an ache in her that she'd never felt before...or since. And it all had centered around J.T. They'd driven through the night, gotten to the chapel across the border at two in the morning, and they'd had to wake up the justice of the peace, a man who appeared more than used to couples turning up on his doorstep in the small hours of the morning.

The music had been a tape, the witness had been the man's wife, and the flowers had been fake. But none of that had mattered, not when she'd been holding on to J.T. and heard the justice of the peace pronounce them man and wife.

None of that mattered until the cold light of morning hit—that, and the fact that they had to go back to face her family. "Damn it all," she muttered in the confines of the elevator car.

When had the fear settled in her? When had she first known that it had all been a crazy, wild dream? When had she realized that she was waking up from it, and J.T. wasn't going to be there with her? She closed her eyes tightly. She knew the answer to all of those questions.

The minute she'd told J.T. she should go home alone, that she could meet him in Dallas later, that she'd have to figure out how to tell her parents what she'd done. She'd seen the look in his hazel eyes. The heat and desire was gone, and in its place had been a hardness she'd never seen before.

That was the moment, even before he told her she either came with him, or she could go back and it was over. Those words had only solidified it. The man didn't bluff. He never did. And he hadn't been bluffing then.

"I don't have time to wait for you to grow up," he'd said, the drawl less pronounced, his words harder and blunt. *"Go home, do what a Montgomery does, and we'll pretend this never happened. That should be easy for you."*

Each word he'd uttered had cut her deeply, but she hadn't been able to stop them any more than she could have turned her back on everything she was and gone off to Dallas with him right then. Not that she hadn't wanted to. Not that she hadn't ached with the need to just hold on to him and have him make everything right. But he wasn't a miracle worker, and nothing would have made their relationship right.

She took a ragged breath and stood up straight as the elevator doors opened. She thought she was in control. She thought she could walk out of the elevator, get a cab, go back to the estate and wait for eight o'clock in the morning to get this finished. But as the doors slid open, she came face-to-face with Karl.

For most of her life, Karl had been there, in the background, unassuming, doting on Whitney and always knowing the right thing to say. But this time he didn't say a thing. He took one look at her, came toward her, then he was hugging her. He'd never done that before, yet it seemed so right for her at that moment.

She was being held gently, the scent of his after-shave soothing as it mingled with the mellowness of cigar smoke that clung to him. She held on to him, and he let her.

J.T. TURNED AS SOON AS the door closed and he headed back to the phone. He picked up the receiver, but Davis was the only one on the line. "Jacob had an emergency arise. He said he'd get right back to us if he could."

"Do you know anyone else who can fill in, someone who would know about Nevada law?"

"Civil?"

"Annulments and marriages."

"I've heard that Zack Taylor is good. He'd know whatever you need to know."

"Okay, call Jacob and leave a message to forget it, then get Taylor and have him call me here right away. I don't care what time it is when you find him."

"Yes, sir."

"And cancel my flight to London."

"Okay, and when do you want it rescheduled for?"

"I don't know right now."

"The meeting's set for ten, sir, and if you don't get a flight out soon, you won't make it in time."

He knew what he was going to do. "I can't make it after all. I trust you to handle it for me."

He heard a slight intake of air on the other end of the phone, but Davis spoke with his usual reserve. "Sir, if you believe that I can handle it, I'd be more than happy to take on the challenge."

"You know everything I know, and you know what I want. If you run into trouble, use the old, 'I

have to check with the legal department,' get the
hell out of there, and contact me on the cell phone.''

"Yes, sir. I'm on the 6:00 a.m. flight out. I'll have
Taylor contact you right away. I've got his home
phone number.''

"Good, Davis, good.''

"Will you be at the hotel?''

"Tell him to try this number, and if I'm not here,
use the cell phone number. Tell him I need everything he has on the annulment proceedings in Nevada.''

"Yes, sir,'' Davis said. "Is there anything else?''

He killed the urge to say, "Sic 'em, boy,'' but
said, "Find out if there's still an Empire Hotel on
the state line.'' He had no idea how he remembered
that or why he even asked the man to find the information.

"Yes, sir. Anything else?''

"Just contact Taylor,'' he said and hung up.

He turned to the room, an incredibly empty room
without Candice in it. The Empire Hotel. Room 227.
That came from nowhere.

He moved to the bed, sank onto the mussed linen
and lay back in the coolness. As he took a deep
breath, he rolled onto his side and was shocked
when he was certain he inhaled Candice's scent. He
could feel a response deep in his soul to the scent,
filtering into him, and he reached for the pillow,
pulling it to his chest.

He'd come to Montgomery Beach with Dylan for
a fling after graduation before he settled into work.
He'd never dreamed that that fling would include
realizing how very crazy he was about his best

friend's sister, or that he'd end up taking her across the state line and marrying her.

A memory of holding her in bed at the Empire Hotel was there, her curled into his embrace, her back against his chest, his arm around her, their legs entwined and that scent everywhere. He could drown in it, let himself go and get lost in the past. But even as he thought it, he knew it was the present too.

His aching need for Candice was very real, and everything in him wanted her right here, in this bed, with him. Because she wanted to be there. Because she wanted him as much as he wanted her. As much as he'd always wanted her.

The phone rang and he rolled to his left and got out of bed. He crossed to the phone and answered it. He expected to hear Davis on the other end and was taken aback by the sound of a familiar voice with a touch of an accent.

"Mr. Watson?" Karl Delaney said.

"Yes. What's wrong?" he asked.

"That is what I was going to ask you."

"I don't—"

"Sir, I just saw Candice off in a cab."

She wasn't with Mark. That surprised him, and pleased him in some way. "Thanks for the report, but what does that have to do with me?"

"She was upset. At least, she seemed to be. When I asked her what was wrong, she said she was fine, but that she needed to get home. It seems she has an appointment early in the morning with you."

He didn't understand, not any more than he understood why she would tell anyone, least of all Karl Delaney.

The line was quiet for a moment, then Karl said, "After our talk, then finding Candice upset, and seeing…" He hesitated, then said, "I knew years ago that there was something between the two of you. Now it appears, at least to me, that there still is."

Damn it, the man *was* psychic, or at least the best observer of people he'd ever met. "Where are you going with this, sir?"

"Simply put, I will not tolerate Candice being deliberately hurt in any way."

"Of course," he said, not about to ask him what business it was of his what he did with Candice or what happened between them.

"You understand what I'm saying to you?"

No, he didn't, not really, or why Karl had even said it. "I wouldn't hurt Candice deliberately. I promise you that."

The man exhaled softly over the line. "And you are a man of your word."

A statement, not a question. "Yes, sir, I am."

"Good. Then do whatever you must do," he said cryptically. "I trust you to do the right thing." Then he hung up.

J.T. slowly lowered the receiver and put it back on the cradle. He shook his head, wondering if he'd fallen down the rabbit hole when he'd come back to Montgomery Beach. In a few short hours, he'd realized mistakes he'd never even considered before, found out that Candice was pretty much the center of the universe for him, that they were still married, and that an older man, who had been the tailor to kings and princes, could read his mind.

The phone rang again and he answered it cau-

tiously, not quite sure who would be on the other
end.

"Yes?"

"Davis here, sir."

He exhaled, relieved that an older man, who had
an uncanny way of seeing things, wasn't on the line.
"Yes, what did you find out?"

"The hotel is still operating. Also, I'm having
trouble locating Taylor, but his wife assured me that
he should be available within the hour. He'll call. Is
there anything else?"

"I think that's it." He hung up, and stood very
still in the center of the room.

*"Do whatever you must do. I trust you to do the
right thing."*

The right thing? Freeing Candice to marry Mark
was the right thing, but it didn't feel right. It was a
noble gesture, no doubt, but it felt all wrong. He
crossed to the windows and everything shifted for
him. Why was he being noble? Candice, a woman
he wanted desperately, was still his wife. And he
was going to hand her over to another man?

That was insane. But she wanted it. And he didn't.
Right then he knew that he wasn't going to be noble.
He was going to do what he wanted to do. He was
going to spend time with Candice and see if there
was any way they could start all over. If there was
any way they could pick up where they left off. If
there was any way they had a future.

But she had made it clear she didn't want to be
around him. She wouldn't even stay in this room to
wait for the attorney to explain things for them. She
was terrified of being with him, and he hoped
against hope it was because she still wanted him. He

knew how much that had scared her before, and maybe, despite the maturity that should have come in eight years, she was still scared.

He was going to count on that. He was going to do whatever it took to get her close to him for at least twenty-four hours. They had had twenty-four hours together eight years ago and she'd left. He'd make sure that the next twenty-four hours with her wouldn't end the same way.

He paced the room, thinking, trying to work out things in his mind, and when the phone rang, he answered it. It was Taylor, and J.T. asked him exactly what he needed to know. When he hung up, he had a set plan. A twenty-four-hour plan. And if it worked, it would change his life. If it didn't work, he knew his life would still be changed, but he'd be alone.

He paced back and forth with a bad case of the jitters. He couldn't sit, he couldn't stay still, and sleeping was out of the question.

He took one look at the bed, and could almost see Candice there, snuggled into the sheets, her blue eyes shining. No, he wasn't going to do much sleeping tonight, he admitted, and reached for his shirt. If he was going to pull this off, he had to be clear-headed, and being in a room where all he had to do was narrow his eyes and he could see her, wasn't the answer.

He put on his boots, reached for his cell phone and wallet, then left, leaving behind the scent of Candice in the air.

CANDICE AWOKE with a start to a dark room and no idea what time it was or when she'd finally fallen asleep. She turned in the huge four-poster bed and saw the low glow from the alarm. Six o'clock. She rolled back over, then pushed herself up. Why had she agreed to meet J.T. this morning? She should have insisted on him meeting with her attorney…if she had an attorney. And why had she told Karl about this meeting?

The man was so comforting last night, just being there for her, not asking for or demanding any explanations, and the only thing she'd thought to tell him was that she was tired, that she had to get home because she had an early appointment with J.T. She could have lied, or she could have just kept her mouth shut.

She pushed herself up in the tangle of sheets that were around her legs, and raked both hands through her hair. She had such a sense of dread about today that she wished she could just go back to sleep and wake tomorrow when everything was over.

A knock on the door startled her and she called out, "Come in."

She expected Noreen, the maid, to be there with coffee and toast, but instead her mother came into the room. Grace was usually up and dressed very early in the morning, every hair in place, her makeup perfect, ready to face the world in total control.

But Candice was taken aback to see her mother still in her long, white silk robe with a discreet *M* embroidered in ivory on the white. Without makeup she looked almost fragile. She silently crossed the room, passing Candice in her bed to go to the French doors that opened onto the balcony. She tugged back the heavy drapes to let faint sunlight into the room.

"Good morning, Candice," she said in a slightly breathy voice as she turned. "I received the strangest call last night."

"What was it?"

"Mr. Delaney, he called to make sure you had gotten home safely. He mentioned something about a taxi and Mark leaving you at the hotel."

"Mark had to leave, some business came up, and Karl took pity on me and called me a cab." She had never been so thankful for the man's quiet gentleness. No questions, no prodding, just a momentary peacefulness in a life that seemed tossed by storms since J.T.'s appearance. She'd been very grateful to have him there, and that she hadn't done what she'd wanted to do right then. Cry again. "I don't know why he would have called you, though."

"He seemed concerned." She twisted the tie of her robe around and around one slender finger. "I had heard you come in, so I knew you were here. And that you were all right."

"He's so nice," she said sincerely. "He's been around for as long as I can remember and he's so...so calm, isn't he?"

Grace looked a bit taken aback with that assessment. "Calm? Yes, I guess he is."

A calm she'd needed last night, and a calm that had lasted until she was in this room alone. Then sleep wouldn't come and her mind hadn't shut down, not when she knew that at eight o'clock this morning, she had to face J.T. again. But for the last time. Then she could get on with her life.

Her mother crossed to her and lightly touched her cheek with a cool hand. "Why is this the first time that I noticed you have a way of frowning that is very much like your father? There are so many things…'' She shook her head, then drew her hand back. ''I'm being silly,'' she murmured.

Candice could see sadness in her eyes, something that had lingered there for what seemed forever, and she wondered what sort of love her parents had had. Certainly not a passionate love, or one that had come and gone in twenty-four hours. Maybe there had been a passion, a needing of each other somewhere in their past, she thought as she got out of bed. ''You miss him, don't you?'' she asked.

''Excuse me?'' Grace asked, stepping back a bit.

''Father, you miss him.''

Grace was very still, then said softly, ''Yes, I do,'' before she shook her head as if to clear her thoughts. ''Can we do lunch today?'' she asked abruptly.

''Lunch?'' She was so used to her mother having her club meetings at lunch or her charity functions that it seemed odd for Grace to be asking to have lunch with her. ''Well, yes, sure, if you'd like?''

''I'd like to. Let's meet at La Maison at one. How's that for you?''

''Good. That's good.''

''I'll look forward to it,'' Grace said, then crossed to the door. Candice felt very alone as the door shut behind her mother. She crossed to the dressing area and tried to decide what to wear, but shivered slightly as she realized that it mattered little what she wore today.

She spotted a simple black pant suit. As she slipped on the pleated slacks and the fitted jacket worn over a white shell, she looked at herself. Definitely the right thing to wear to the burial of her past.

Chapter Twelve

J.T. stood in the lobby of the hotel, leaning against one of the stone pillars by the reception desk. His Stetson was tugged low over his eyes, but he made very sure he could see the entry and out onto the loop under the portico where the guests arrived. He was five minutes early, and that had been a real ordeal to achieve. He'd been awake since five, so restless that he'd gotten on the phone and gone over specifics for the meeting with Davis. Things that made no difference, but things that distracted him from what he was going to attempt to do in the next twenty-four hours.

He straightened when a black Mercedes coupe pulled up to the curb, then exhaled when an elderly lady got out and handed her keys to the valet. It was then that he realized he had no idea what car Candice would be driving. Eight years ago she'd driven a bright red Jeep, but that hardly seemed like something she'd drive now.

Even as he thought it, he saw her. She pulled up to the entrance in a midnight-blue BMW coupe. Sleek and understated, just the way she looked now.

If you didn't look behind the veneer. He stood straight, not going to meet her, just watching.

Wife.

The word had meant little to J.T. eight years ago. He'd just known that whatever they had was explosive and the need for her had been beyond compelling. Yet there was something there, something that had stopped him from taking what she'd offered. Something that felt the unsteadiness in her when he touched her, that slight shadow in her eyes that in some way made him feel protective and.... He shrugged, the word not there for him, even now.

Whatever it had been, he knew that marriage was what she'd needed, and he'd gone along with it. Rational thought hadn't been his strong suit that weekend. Not when she'd laced her fingers with his, moved so close, her body heat had scorched him, and her lips were sweeter than anything he'd ever tasted before in his life. No rational thought had had any place in their world that weekend. At least not at the beginning.

He watched her move in a simple black pant suit that was modest and obviously expensive. Yet there was that swelling of her hips, the way the jacket seemed to mold to her high breasts. She nibbled on her bottom lip as she handed the keys to the valet. He took a deep, unsteady breath, willing himself not to react to her presence in an obvious way, then she looked up and he knew she saw him.

For one fleeting moment, he felt such a connection that it rocked him. What he was going to do was right, he thought, as those blue eyes met his and he could feel a current between them. But Candice didn't show it if the contact affected her the same way. She skimmed her gaze over him, taking in his jeans, boots, pale blue shirt and Stetson. With a slight nod of acknowledgment, she walked out of the sunlight, into the lobby and toward him as if he was some business acquaintance she was there to meet.

He wasn't given to self-doubt, just doing what he had to do. Yet he could feel uncertainty in him at that moment, something he seldom felt in business, and never in his personal life...until now. He pushed it aside and walked toward her, meeting her almost in the middle of the lobby. Whatever he was doing, he had to do it. If he didn't, there was nothing. Candice with Mark, and him... He didn't even know where he'd be if that happened.

"Good morning, darlin'. I wasn't sure you'd come," he said, consciously trying to be casual and not give away the fact that the thought of her not showing up had kept him up for a good portion of a very long night.

"Of course I came," she said, any softness in her voice obliterated by her next words. "We both want this over with as quickly as possible."

Her words jarred him, and he looked away from her, past her to the BMW being driven away from the curb by the valet. "Of course," he said.

She came a step closer. "Let's find someplace that's not so public."

"I've still got a room here," he said.

Her expression tightened. "I'm sure we can find someplace down here to talk."

He motioned to the plaza. "How about outside? It's early. Not too many people are up and around yet."

She hesitated, then nodded and started to walk to the doors that led to the plaza. He fell in step beside her, being very careful not to brush arms as they walked. Any contact just yet wouldn't be a good idea, for either one of them.

They were out the doors, onto the stone patio area, and one look around told him he'd been right. There wasn't a person in sight. He stopped when she did by a series of small metal tables to one side. Candice sat down, laid down a small black purse he hadn't noticed her carrying until then, and looked right at him with those incredible blue eyes.

"Okay, what did you find out and what do we have to do?" she said.

He took off his Stetson and laid it by her purse before he started to tell her his version of what Taylor had told him only hours ago. "An annulment in this state won't be fast at all. Since it's been eight years, it's a legal nightmare. And a divorce, well, even if we went that route, it's very time-consuming."

She leaned forward and lowered her voice. "I don't care what it is, a divorce or an annulment, but we need to do it now."

"That's exactly my point. We can't."

She frowned, drawing a fine line between her blue eyes. "You said last night that we could do this and get it over with."

"I told you, anything done in California will take time, and if you plan on marrying anytime soon, don't." He sort of enjoyed the way her chin was coming up a bit as he spoke. "What Taylor said was, we're talking at least six months. That's uncontested, plain and simple, no complications. No

property to divide, and no kids to decide custody
of.''

''That's it?''

''No, it's not. There are alternatives, and since
you need this done quickly, Taylor figured out a way
to have it done in a day or two. If you're willing to
do your part.''

She narrowed her eyes on him. ''Where are you
going with this?''

''To Nevada. Across the border.''

The frown gave way to pure puzzlement. ''What
are you talking about?''

''What part of Nevada or across the border didn't
you understand, darlin'?''

''All of it,'' she said through clenched teeth.

''If you want this done quickly, the only way to
do it is to do it in Nevada, across the border. It's a
three-day deal that Taylor says can be cut to a day
and a half if he contacts the right people. No long
waiting period, no delays, just a neat, simple annulment or divorce.''

The frown was gone, and as she sat back, she
looked relieved. ''That's it?''

''That's it.''

Her tongue touched her lips, an action that didn't
help him stay calm. Then blue eyes were on him
again. ''Okay, let's do it. Tell Taylor to get on it
and get it done.''

''I didn't say Taylor could do it.''

''You just said—''

''That if he contacts the right people, he can cut
the time frame to a day and a half.''

''I don't understand.''

"By law, the interested parties, you and me, have to be there ourselves to do the actual deed."

She stared at him, the color in her face draining so alarmingly that he was afraid she was going to pass out again. But instead, she took a ragged breath and said, "You think... Are you saying that we...we have to..."

"Exactly," he said with a nod.

She stared at him, the cool light of morning touching her paleness with little color. For a single moment he considered stopping his plan, telling her that Taylor could take care of it in a matter of weeks, but he stopped himself from doing it. He could be dead wrong about everything, but he had to try.

She lifted her chin a fraction of an inch and the control was back. "If you think we're going to Nevada together, you're crazy."

"It's your choice. Either do this, or put off whatever you have planned with your yuppie fiancé for a considerable amount of time. It's nothing to me."

Candice stared hard at the Stetson on the table, then back at the man who had been wearing it. The morning light wasn't kind, exposing fine lines at his eyes and mouth, and it did little to hide the look in those hazel eyes. *"It's nothing to me."* Well, it meant a hell of a lot to her, but taking off for Nevada with J.T. wasn't an option.

"There has to be another way of doing it and doing it quickly."

"If you figure it out, let me know. I don't have time to mess around with this, darlin'."

"Stop doing that," Candice said before she knew she was even going to say it.

J.T. raised one eyebrow. ''Stop doing what, dar-lin'?''

''That. Calling me darling.'' She couldn't tell him how that made her feel, because she didn't understand it herself.

He shrugged. ''Sorry about that, darl—'' He smiled at that, an expression that crinkled his hazel eyes and tugged at his lips. And she wished he'd stop that too. It made it too damn hard to really think. ''Sorry…Ms. Montgomery.''

That teasing just never stopped. ''You never stop, do you?''

He sobered completely, his eyes direct and intense. ''Not until I want to,'' he murmured.

She shivered slightly and tightened her body to try to control it. ''Whatever,'' she muttered. ''We just need to get this done, so we can both get on with our lives.'' Suddenly she realized that her life, in some subtle way, had been on hold for eight years, even though she hadn't known it. Eight long years. And she wanted it back. She wanted to breathe without a catch in her chest and to wake in the morning without that vague feeling of something hanging over her head. ''We just need to get this done.''

''Then you know how to do that.''

She hadn't planned on going back to any part of eight years ago. But that was a joke. Last night she'd been dangerously close to slipping back to that fool who had let her heart rule her head, the fool who had thought that when a man offered to marry you, when that man took you away to get married, he loved you and would be there no matter what. A fool. Her stomach clenched.

"Okay, you go there as soon as you can. Let me know where it is, and I'll go and sign the papers, and that's that," she said, feeling pleased with her plan.

"What are you talking about?" he asked.

"Just what you said. You go ahead and do what you need to do. Then go off to London or Paris or wherever you're needed. I'll settle things here, then go and do my part."

"That's not acceptable."

Her nerves were raw, and she knew she couldn't do this much longer. "Not acceptable? What does that mean?"

"It means that either we do this together, or it won't work." He stood, reached for his hat and tugged it low over his eyes. "You and me, across the border. We do it, we finish it, we get out of there."

"I can't just pick up and run off to Nevada with you without…" Her words died off as his expression tightened at an echo of words that had been said eight years ago. She stood, hating the way he towered over her. "I have responsibilities."

"We can't just run off like that," she'd said.

But a kiss had turned her resolve to putty, and a touch had rendered her crazy. *"Darlin', I want you, and I'm not about to hurt you. We can be married in four hours."*

Any protest she'd had in her had been dissolved in his arms, and she'd gone with him. She'd gone across the border, said words about sickness and health, richer or poorer, until death… But it hadn't taken death to part them. Nothing that drastic.

"You're an adult, a grown woman, don't tell me

you're saying you need your family's permission to leave for a day?'' he asked.

"Just come with me. You're my wife. You don't need Daddy's permission to be with me."

He'd never understood why she couldn't just hurt her family and go to Dallas. He'd never understood why she'd had to go back home to talk to them, and to take time to get them used to the idea of a marriage to him.

"It's a mistake," he'd said. *"A complete mistake. You're so tied up with being a Montgomery that you aren't free to be anything, least of all my wife. It's my mistake."* No, he'd never understood, and he'd never loved her. He'd never even come after her.

''I've got responsibilities,'' she repeated with as much calm as she could muster. ''And you've got Vonya. She's expecting you. How will you explain things to her?''

''Not for a week and I'm not telling her a thing about this, not any more than you're planning on telling that yuppie anything.''

''You couldn't just drop everything and come to Dylan's wedding. Well, guess what? I can't just drop everything and run off like that.''

''No, I guess you can't,'' he said with an odd twinge of what she thought could be sadness. But that was foolishness. It wasn't sadness, it had to be impatience or anger or just plain frustration at not getting this over and done with.

He was backing up, slowly, surely. He was leaving. And she knew right then that if he left, this might never get done. She couldn't let that happen. ''Just ask Taylor to do it, and see if he can—''

He didn't say a thing, just turned and headed for

the doors. She hurried after him, reaching him as he
got to the doors. "J.T.?"

He stopped so suddenly that she almost ran into
his back, but she drew away just in time. "Do it
any way you want to do it, darlin', and when I get
the chance, I'll do my end of it. But I can't promise
when that will be." He looked almost grim now.
"I've got my own life to live, and it's not being put
on hold for your convenience."

Those hazel eyes were so cold now, so detached
that it made her nauseous. Why did it matter so
much to her and so little to him? She held her purse
tightly and tried to figure this out. But only one thing
was there. She had to stop what was happening. She
had to control this insanity that came about when-
ever she was around him. And she had to put an end
to it once and for all.

"It would...wouldn't be longer than a day or
two?"

"Taylor said thirty-six hours, tops, but most
likely twenty-four hours."

Any length of time alone with him would be impossible, but then she realized that it wasn't impossible. A day or so of being in Nevada, putting in the
time, then signing the papers and that was that. They
wouldn't have to stay at the same hotel, just be in
the same state.

"You promise it won't be longer?"

"All I need is twenty-four hours, cross my
heart."

"Okay," she said, getting out the single word
quickly before she could think any more about it.
Damn it, the smile came back, but only a suggestion
of what she knew it could be.

"Good decision," he said. "Now, let's go. We can either rent a car or take yours. It's your choice."

"We can take my car to the airport."

"No airport. The only flight that would work isn't until late this afternoon at four."

"Fine. That gives me time to pack and—"

"We have to meet Taylor there at two. So, that's not an option." He came a bit closer, keeping his voice low. "So, do we drive?"

"We'll charter a flight then," she said quickly.

"Tried. All gone. None available from here." A smile was playing at his lips, a smile of a winner and she hated it. "Do we drive or forget about it?"

He was keeping his voice down to keep from being heard by the few guests in the lobby, but to her it only made things more intimate. Something she didn't want any part of with him. "Okay, we'll drive, but I do the driving in my car, and when we get there, we meet Taylor, do whatever we need to do, then I drive back alone. You get a flight out of there or rent a car or something, okay?"

The smile shifted a bit, but it never quite left, and for some reason, she knew this was exactly the way he wanted it to be. "Perfect. Let's go."

She looked down at her suit. "I have to go home and get some things."

"You can buy whatever you need on the way or once we get there." He gestured to a bellhop near the reception desk. "Bring my bag?"

The boy nodded, then reached behind the desk and lifted a small duffel bag. He was already packed and ready to go. She stared at him. He was that sure she'd do what he wanted her to do? Of course he

was. People always did what J.T. wanted them to
do. That was a given. And she was no different.

She hesitated. "This is all going to be absolutely
legal, isn't it?"

He laughed at that, but there wasn't any humor
in the sound now. It sounded cold. "Hell, yes. We
wouldn't want to have to do this again in another
eight years, would we?"

"No," she whispered, wondering how she was
going to survive it this time.

The bellhop was there with his bag, and as J.T.
took it, he looked back at her. "Let's go. We'll just
have time to get there to meet Taylor."

"Okay. But I can't just run off like this." She bit
her lip before she added, "Not again."

She didn't miss the sharpness of his inhaled
breath. "You know what, let's forget this whole
thing. Let it run its course naturally, and sooner or
later it'll be done." He turned away from her, heading into the lobby. "I'll be in touch."

He made things so damn hard. He always had.
The ultimatums, the final lines. Always his way,
even when he said it was up to her. "J.T., stop being
such a jerk," she said as she hurried to catch up to
him.

He stopped abruptly and turned, but instead of
anger, he was almost smiling. "Jerk? I've got things
to do, and I don't have time for this unless we can
leave right now. Do you want this to happen or
not?"

What she wanted was peace. "Yes, I do."

"And you'll leave right now?"

She wished she could think clearly. "Okay, okay,

you win. I can call home from the cell phone to explain why I'm leaving.''

He studied her for a long moment as they stood in the center of the lobby, then said softly, ''You can do that, dar...Candice.''

''Oh, call me whatever you want, and let's do this.''

That smile was back, in his eyes and etching his face. An expression that made her suddenly feel as if she had nothing beneath her feet, and she had to grasp something for balance by touching the nearest chair to steady herself.

''Okay, let's,'' he said.

''You're so damn annoying,'' she said without thinking as she walked away from him. ''Okay, my car, I'm driving. Let's go.''

''Fine, have it your way,'' he replied.

When she reached the door, she stopped and turned to him. ''And quit saying that,'' she said in a chastising whisper, more than aware of other people in the lobby.

''I didn't call you darlin'.''

''Quit saying, 'Have it your way.' None of this is the way I'd do it,'' she said firmly.

''How would you do it?'' he asked, that smile still in his eyes.

''If I could do it my way, I never would have gotten into this mess in the first place. I would have never gone crazy and married you and messed everything up.'' Words hung between them, hard words that she wasn't about to soften.

The smile was gone, as if it had never been, and he leaned so close to her that she felt the heat of his

breath brush her face when he whispered tightly,
"Nothing was done against your will."

She stared into his hazel eyes. No, she'd wanted
it, wanted him beyond anything she'd ever wanted
before. She just never dreamed that she'd live to
regret it so much. "You're right, I was just plain
crazy," she retorted and continued out the door toward valet parking.

She didn't have to turn to know he was coming
with her, walking almost beside her. She didn't stop
until she was at the valet pick-up spot. The kid
working the station saw her and headed off to get
her car. J.T. was beside her, not saying a thing, and
she wasn't about to say anything else. She stared at
the attendant running into a side parking lot to head
for her BMW.

By the time the car was pulling up in front of
them, the silence between them was almost painful.
She went around to get in behind the wheel, handed
the boy a tip, and as soon as J.T. was in the car, she
drove off.

As she got to the main road that led to the freeway, she reached for the car phone and pushed in
the number for her house. It rang twice before going
to the voice mail on her mother's personal line.

"Hi, it's me. Something came up and I'm going
out of town for a few days. I'm sorry about lunch.
I was really looking forward to it, but we can do it
when I get back. I'll call you tonight," she said, then
pressed the end button.

"You got his voice mail?"

She ignored his question as she offered the phone
to him. "Do you need to call anyone?"

He took the phone, and when his fingers brushed

hers, she almost dropped it. She regripped the steering wheel and stared straight ahead, trying very hard not to listen to what he said. But she couldn't block it out.

"Vonya, it's me. I guess by now you figured out I wasn't on the plane with you last night. I got tied up here, and I won't be in London for a day or two. I'll call when I get there," he said, his voice dropping a bit. "I think a vacation is in order after all of this. Later," he said, then hung up.

"All set," he said and she sensed him settling back in the seat. Out of the corner of her eye, she saw his hand rest on the console by the phone, a strong hand, square-tipped fingers. She looked away quickly.

"You got her voice mail, didn't you?" she said, deliberately echoing his own question.

"She's on her way to Saint Tropez to work, so I didn't expect to get her in person," he said.

She fingered the steering wheel. "So, she's... exactly what is she?"

He chuckled at that. "Gorgeous, bright, fun, uncomplicated."

She fought the impulse to look at him. Instead, she stared at the freeway signs, trying to figure out where to go. As if he read her mind, he pointed to one of the signs. "That's our route up to Sacramento, then east to the border." She curved along an off-ramp, then back onto the other freeway that headed east toward the border. "So, what was it you were asking?" he said.

"I know she's a model, but I just wondered what sort. I mean, there's all sorts, I think."

"She does it all." He exhaled. "And she does it well."

"I guess she has a name," she said, hating the innuendo in his last words. Innocent enough words, but said in a way that brought up images of J.T. and Vonya together.

"She has one name, and that name is known all over the world. I'd say she has a name, darlin'."

The word *darlin'* slipped out, and she was finding that it felt a shade comfortable. That worried her until she asked, "What is her last name?"

He shrugged. "I heard it once, but she seldom uses it."

"Why not?"

"I don't know. We never talked about it. But I'll have to ask her," he said. "We just don't do much talkin'," he said on a sly chuckle. "If you get my drift."

"I didn't ask."

"No, but you were wondering, I could tell."

"What in the hell—"

"Whoa, there you go again, using that language. You sound like a ranch hand." She knew he was sitting up a bit straighter and looking right at her. "You have changed, darlin', big time."

"We both have," she said, ignoring that sensation of him staring at her.

"Amen to that, darlin'," he said softly.

Chapter Thirteen

Candice reached over and turned on the radio, letting the sounds of the Beatles fill the spaces and stop any need for further talk between them. She stared straight ahead, driving with the traffic, thankful not to be talking, even though her mind was churning.

The silence between them went unbroken, while J.T. slouched low in the seat, tipping his hat even farther forward to shield his eyes. She had no idea if he was asleep or just biding his time. He didn't move or talk until they passed Sacramento, then she sensed him shift in the seat.

"Darlin', don't forget to get off this freeway and take Route 50. Otherwise, we'll end up in Reno, and Taylor will be waiting for us in Carson City."

She spotted the sign for Route 50 and muttered, "I knew that," even though she'd totally forgotten about the other route she had to take. She made the transition onto the highway, heading west.

She jumped when J.T. turned off the radio right in the middle of "Yesterday" and sat up even more. "Darlin', are you sure you don't want me to drive? You've been at it for almost three hours."

She glanced at him to find him sitting up a bit and pushing his hat back with his thumb.

"I'm fine," she said tightly.

It startled her when her stomach growled, and she pressed one hand to her middle.

"Pardon me?" J.T. drawled.

She wasn't in the mood for jokes. "Did you have breakfast?"

"I didn't have time. How about you?"

She hadn't even thought of food before meeting him. "No, I didn't have time, either." Now the hunger was very real. She looked around at the stretches of open land that led up to the low foothills then the mountains and into Nevada. "We can find someplace up the road and get something to eat. We'll have time, won't we?"

"Sure, it won't take long. And I'm starved. You know," he said, looking around them. "I think there's a place up about five miles or so," J.T. said. "At least there used to be. Hank's Watering Hole. Remember that place?"

He'd asked that so casually, as if he'd just thought of it, but she wasn't so blasé. She couldn't stop her foot from jerking on the gas, or the car from lurching. Taking a breath, she steadied herself and the car. She'd forgotten—or maybe tried to forget—all about that place. The flashing neon lights framing the roadhouse, the flashing blue Vacancy sign high above a semicircle courtyard motel behind it, and the trucks parked everywhere.

Yes, she remembered the place, remembered going inside, ordering, then being so anxious to get going, they'd had the food packaged to go. "It's near here?'' she asked, hearing the tightness in her own voice.

''Should be. How about stopping there to pick up some food?''

She shook her head, not anxious to revisit any more of the past than she had to. ''I don't think so. There're probably tons of other places around to get something to eat.''

''Oh sure, of course, I get it. I remember now. You saying something last time about it be-ing…what was your word, seedy? And you called it a roadhouse, I think. And your nose crinkled with distaste and you probably shivered delicately.''

He was making fun of her and she couldn't stand it. ''That's not fair,'' she said tightly, hating the edge of humor. ''It was…well, it seemed sort of…''

''Seedy?''

''Okay, seedy. Does that make you happy to hear me say it?''

''Whoa there, hold on. I don't want to do battle over this. We need food. If you find another place before we get to it, forget about Hank's. Hell, it might not even be there anymore. But if it is, if you don't feel you can stop there, keep going.''

Truth be told, she was starved, and she would stop just about anywhere to eat. But he'd almost dared her to stop there. She could. It was only a place. And, as he said, it might not even be there. But as she looked ahead, she realized it was there, very much there.

The huge sign that pushed over thirty feet into the sky proclaimed, Hank's Watering Hole, and under that another sign, Last Chance for Good Food and Good Music Before You Leave California. Then she saw the place itself. In the afternoon sunlight, the glittery honky-tonk look had been replaced by an almost weary look, all backdropped by rolling fields of something very green, sprawling back toward the low foothills.

The main building's red paint was oxidized, and the ring of cottages matched it. Trucks were parked in rows in front of the complex, more of them by a multidoor garage to the west, and smoke came out of a vent in the center of the main building's roof. It wasn't night, and the lights weren't flashing, and this wasn't eight years ago. It was now, and this was just a place to get food.

"I'll be damned, darlin', it's still there," J.T. drawled. "So, how about it? It still isn't up to Montgomery standards, but if I remember correctly, the food's passable and the music is very interesting."

She flinched internally at his jab about Montgomery standards and looked at the situation logically. It was just a place. That was all. "Food is food," she said and turned off the highway onto a narrow frontage road that led into the graveled parking lot.

"Good choice," J.T. said.

The gravel crunched under the tires of the BMW as Candice drove between idling big rigs toward the front of the main building. She pulled into a slot between two of the large trucks, then turned off the engine. As she undid her seat belt, she looked at J.T. "Food and drinks to go, then we leave, right?"

"Absolutely," J.T. said before he got out of the car.

Candice got out into the warm June day and headed toward the entry doors. She'd called it a roadhouse, and that's what it looked like, down to and including the heavyset man at the front door welcoming people. A bouncer. He looked like one and acted like one, checking out people going inside. "Good day to you," he said.

J.T. touched the brim of his Stetson. "Nice day."

"That it is," the man said, reaching to open the door for them.

Candice went inside first, into the mingled scent of barbecue and sawdust, the mingled noises of a pool hall to one side, a main section playing loud western music, where some couples were dancing a Texas two-step, to the restaurant section on the far side. The mixture of noises and smells triggered a memory of walking through the place with J.T. before, his arm around her, both of them anxious to get their food and keep going. But then it had been to get married, now it was to undo that marriage.

Then she'd been in jeans and a sweater, not a name-brand suit, and running shoes, not black pumps. Her outfit didn't fit here any more than she did. But J.T. fit in perfectly.

"Candice, the man is at home with horses and stable hands," her father had said once. *"Even all that money does₁ t compensate for lack of breeding. Nothing can change that or make him fit in at the better places."*

She kept walking toward the food area, cringing inwardly at the memory of those words. Her father had been so cold then. Caring, but distant and so judgmental. She'd never thought about him like that before, but now that she did, she could admit that a lot of what J.T. had said about him was true. She'd been automatically defensive, but back then she

hadn't had any defense for the way both her mother
and father treated people out of their circle.

She reached the counter, slipped onto one of the
revolving stools and felt J.T. sit beside her. How
dare they judge people, as if they were the standard-
bearers of the civilized world.

Good heavens, that was exactly what J.T. had said
to her so long ago. *"How can they set themselves
up to judge others, as if they're the standard-bearers
of the civilized world?"* She had no idea she'd remembered that until now. Or felt so in agreement
with what he said. At the time J.T. had said that to
her, she'd been furious and defensive. But there was
no defense for what her parents had done.

She couldn't even look at J.T., not while being
overwhelmed by a strange need to apologize to him
for something she'd said or done so long ago. A
sense of guilt settled heavily on her as she glanced
up at the menu scrawled on a large chalkboard at-
tached to the wall behind the counter.

J.T. moved, brushing against her, and she stiff-
ened. Why was she so bothered by what her father
had said long ago? She'd never even questioned it.
The truth was there. She should have questioned it.
She should have stood up to her father and mother
and told them how wrong they'd been. She should
have defended J.T. to them.

It was too late for all of this soul-searching, these
belated admissions. The fact was, J.T. would be out
of her life in less than twenty-four hours and he
wouldn't look back. He didn't care. That's why he'd
been so calm in the face of her mother's snubs last
night. He didn't care.

She glanced at him, at his hat pulled low, the

jeans tight and well-worn. He did what he wanted. He didn't care. He fit in here, and he fit in at the ranch, but he fit in in a board room and at Montgomery Beach. She felt a real remorse that she'd let her parents' prejudice color her thoughts to the extent that she'd been terrified to tell them that she loved J.T.

He was talking to her, saying something that she hadn't even heard. And he was looking expectantly at her, as if he was waiting for her to say something. But all she could think of was being sorry. "I'm sorry," she said out loud, more sorry than he'd ever know for what she'd allowed and done eight years ago.

"That's okay, I was just asking you what you want."

"You," she almost said, but bit her lip hard and turned to the menu on the board. Food. That's what he was talking about. She had loved him, really loved him, and hadn't even known it. Or she hadn't let herself know it, the fear of what would have happened in her family if she'd acknowledged that love just too great back then. "A turkey sandwich," she said.

Then she looked at J.T., at a face that had never left her heart, and a truth exploded in her with the impact of a nuclear bomb. She *still* loved him, really loved him. And that knowledge all but suffocated her.

"Are you okay?" J.T. asked, leaning closer to her and only making things worse.

She hadn't been "okay" for eight years.

"Darlin', you look green around the gills," J.T. said. "You need food."

She needed him. God help her, but she needed him, and here he was bound and determined to get an annulment. "I'm hungry," she managed to say finally.

"Damn straight. Now for the big question."

She swallowed hard to get out a single word. "What?"

The hazel eyes were shadowed by his hat, but the impact of the gaze was strong and sure with that glimmer of humor in their depths. "Wheat or white?" He grinned at her and her heart lurched. "I don't know that much about you, despite being married to you for eight years."

He was making a joke about something that didn't mean a thing to him, but it hurt her to the core. "Wheat, and...coffee with it, black."

"Okay, wheat and black. Got it," he said and turned to the waitress again.

She stared at J.T., at the strong profile, at the way he slipped off the Stetson and laid it on the stool on his other side. Then he raked his fingers through his hair and laughed with the waitress. Her husband. Candice swiveled her stool abruptly away from him. Love. God help her, she *did* love him. She ached for him, and for eight years that ache had been buried under mountains of denial and fear. But it was there now, strong and undeniable.

She could hear him talking to the waitress, then the girl was saying, "Well, cowboy, you smile at me like that, and I'll forget the tax on your meal."

Candice knew what that smile did to people, what it did to her. The air was thin in the room and she felt flushed. She slipped off the stool, and without looking at J.T., said, "I'm going to the rest room," then walked off on decidedly shaky legs.

She wended her way through the crowd, got into the rest room, a single space where she could lock the door and be alone. She clicked the lock in place, then leaned against the tile wall. She loved him. She closed her eyes tightly, taking some deep, unsteady breaths. And she didn't know what to do.

Everything was out of kilter. Including her relationship with Mark. She exhaled as she realized that that part of her life was over. In a flash it had gone. She couldn't marry him. She couldn't marry anyone. J.T. had torn up her life again. He'd even offered to get the annulment as a wedding present for the two of them.

She crossed to the sink and ran cold water, cupping it in her hands and splashing it on her face. She couldn't marry Mark. She was married to J.T. She loved J.T. In any reasonable situation, that would be perfect. But this wasn't a reasonable situation. Not any more than it had been eight years ago.

Eight years ago, all she would have to do was tell J.T. she loved him, and she'd be with him no matter what anyone thought or said. But she hadn't said either thing. Now, eight years later, the words were there. She loved him, and she knew that she'd go anywhere with him and whatever her mother thought wouldn't stop that. Eight years later, she was finally mature and knew exactly what she wanted.

She reached for a paper towel, sponged at her face, then looked at herself in the mirror. She looked as tense as she felt. Eight years were gone, but she had now. She had this moment, and if she could get up the courage, she could say what she felt. Tell the truth, then hope that things would work out. This time. Finally.

Just the simple truth. She tossed the paper towel in the waste basket. She'd tell J.T. that she didn't want the annulment, she didn't want him to leave, she didn't want him to walk out of her life. She loved him. Simple. Just do it, she told herself, knowing that the worst that could happen—that J.T. would walk away—was no worse than what would happen if she said nothing.

She started to smooth her hair, but her hands were shaking so much she gave up. She felt as nervous as she had eight years ago when she'd left Montgomery Beach with J.T. There was a pounding on the door and someone calling, "Hey, are you finished in there?"

She looked at herself. Finished? No, nothing was finished, not yet. She opened the door and hurried past two ladies waiting to use the rest room, then turned to go into the main part of the restaurant. She looked ahead at the counter to where J.T. was sitting and talking to the waitress again. No, not just talking. He was laughing, and the woman was obviously charmed. Women were charmed by J.T., she had been. She still was.

Then she remembered Vonya. The way Vonya had acted around J.T., the flirting and giggling. The lipstick on J.T. after they'd said goodbye. Maybe this wouldn't be so simple.

She went toward him, and when she was close enough to see the way his hair curled slightly at the collar of his shirt, J.T. turned. Those hazel eyes were on her, then that smile was there, an expression that turned her world on its ear.

"Well, darlin', you're back." The smile faded a bit. "Are you feeling any better?"

She nodded, taking her seat again. "Sure, I'm okay." How was she going to do this? Just blurt out "I love you," and wait for the reaction? She sat forward, resting her elbows on the countertop. No, she'd wait. They had over an hour of driving before getting to Carson City, over an hour to get the right opening, then do what she should have done eight years ago.

J.T. touched her shoulder, and she turned to him. "What?"

He motioned to a disposable cup of coffee the waitress had set in front of her. "Maybe some coffee will help."

She stared at the coffee, wishing there was some way she could pick the cup up right then, but she couldn't trust her hands to be steady enough not to spill the hot liquid. "In a while," she said.

"When you get some food in your stomach, you'll feel better," J.T. said with that easy smile. A smile she loved.

J.T. WAS GETTING WORRIED about Candice, and worried about what he was doing. He never second-guessed his decisions, but right then he was close to doing exactly that. She looked ready to fly apart, all edgy and nervous. He didn't miss the unsteadiness in her hands that cradled the coffee cup.

Maybe he'd been wrong to do this, to all but force her to come with him, then keep up the pretence that Taylor was meeting them across the border.

There would be no Taylor, and if he had his way, no annulment, but that was up to Candice. Everything was up to Candice, and for the first time in his life he felt helpless.

"Why is it taking so long?" Candice asked in a voice so low he almost didn't hear her.

Stopping here hadn't been a good idea, after all. He'd almost dared her to stop, hoping that it would bring back some good memories. But now he knew it had been a mistake. Ever since they'd stepped inside, she'd looked as if she was going to be sick. He stopped himself from touching her to steady her. "It'll be ready soon, then we can get going." He added a lie to it. "We'll make our appointment with Taylor easily. So, don't worry."

That only made her pale even more. "J.T., maybe we shouldn't have done this," she said softly.

"Done what? Gotten married? Forgotten to get it annulled, or come in here?"

That paleness became even more pronounced. "Everything," she said with a sigh, and he didn't miss the way she pressed a hand to her middle.

"If you're going to be sick—"

"I'm not."

"Maybe you had too much to drink last night?"

"No, it's not that," she murmured, exhaling on a shaky rush.

"Car sickness?"

"No, of course not."

"You're getting the flu?"

She grimaced at that. "I'm not sick."

"Then tell me what's going on."

Her eyes flicked past him to the room at large, then back to him. "Not here."

Thankfully, the waitress was suddenly there holding a white bag. "Here you go, folks," she said, handing the bag to J.T. along with the bill. "That'll be twelve dollars."

J.T. took out a twenty and laid it on the counter. "Thanks for everything," he said, then turned to Candice, but she and her coffee were gone.

He looked up and saw her walking out of the dining area and into the dance space. He picked up his coffee and the bag of food and hurried after her. By the time he caught up with her, she was at the entry where the door was being held open for her by the bouncer.

"Have a good day, ma'am," the bulky man said with a smile, and with a nod, she passed by and out into the sunlight.

J.T. walked outside while the man held the door open, then looked up and Candice was almost to the car. By the time he caught up with her, she was at the front of the car. She stopped, waiting without turning. Then he was beside her, and she looked up at him, the true blue of her eyes exposed by the sunlight.

He feigned being out of breath. "What are you training for, one of those marathons?"

He'd meant to make a joke, to take some of the strain off her face, but it didn't work. "We need to get out of here," she said.

"I'm driving," he said.

She hesitated, then surprisingly didn't argue. She held the key out to him, and he went around to the passenger side.

He got in behind the wheel, put his coffee in the nearest holder and closed the door. By the time he turned on the ignition, Candice was in the seat beside him, rustling the bag to get out her sandwich. He backed out, turned and headed toward the highway that would take them through the mountains and to the border.

He put out his hand. "Food. I need food."

She fumbled in the bag and took out his sandwich. "Can you eat it while you drive?"

He laughed. "I can eat while I'm driving, riding a horse or just plain walking," he said. "No problem. Just give me half of it." He held out his hand, and when she put the half sandwich in it, he could feel her shaking. He didn't look at her, but took a bite of the sandwich and drove out onto the frontage road, then back onto the highway heading east.

He ate without really tasting, all of his attention on the woman so close to him. He waved away the second half of the sandwich and drank the coffee as the road started to climb. Finally, after glancing at Candice and seeing her sandwich unwrapped on her lap, but barely touched, he'd had enough.

"Okay, you said you'd tell me what's going on," But he wasn't at all sure he wanted to know.

She took her time rewrapping the barely touched sandwich and pushed it into the bag. When she reached for her coffee in the holder, he could see her hand was shaking. She drew back, not taking the coffee, and he heard a heavy sigh. "I'm not sure where to start."

"Start where you want to start, darlin', I'm a captive audience," he said, gripping the steering wheel so tightly his hands were aching.

"This…this Taylor person who's meeting us there, what's he going to do exactly?"

He stuck with the truth, or what it would have been if Taylor was actually going to meet them. "Bring the papers, get them notarized, etcetera, etcetera, etcetera."

"Can you get a hold of him?"

"Are you worried he won't show up?"

"No, I just…" She exhaled. "J.T., are you going to marry Vonya?"

That shocked him. "Me, marry Vonya? I'm not planning on marrying anyone. Been there, done that. Why would you ask that?"

"You're in such a rush to get the annulment, I mean, just taking off and making that man meet us there, and pushing everything through."

"You're the one getting married. You're the one who needs the annulment to make you a free person so you don't commit bigamy, which, by the way, either one of us could have committed in the past eight years and not even known it."

He heard her take a shaky breath before she said, "You know, we don't have to do this."

He thought he hadn't heard her right. "What?"

"We don't have to rush. It seems so…so hasty. I mean, it's been eight years, and we just found out, and what if we don't do it right?"

He glanced at her and found her looking right at him, twisted in the seat to look at him more squarely. She wasn't saying what he thought she was saying. It couldn't happen this easily. "Where did that come from?"

She leaned toward him slightly. "The first time we rushed everything. We barely had time to even figure out what we were doing, just taking off, and the next thing we knew, it was done. It was so fast."

It had been like lightning, brilliant and all-encompassing, and gone as quickly as it had come. "Like catching lightning in a bottle," he murmured.

"Yes, and just as impossible."

"I don't understand."

"J.T., I don't want to make a horrible mistake again. I want things to be right. I want to—" Her words were cut off by a scream when she looked ahead of them.

For a split second he didn't understand, then he turned and saw a truck coming right at them. Life slowed to a frame-by-frame existence, Candice screaming, him realizing they were on the wrong side of the road, pulling the wheel to the right, the rumbling rush of the truck barely missing them as the BMW went into a spin. But any relief was short-lived when he saw nothing but air, an impossibility unless they were going over the side, and the car was sailing through space.

The world froze, there was just the two of them, and his last glimpse was of Candice looking at him, and his last thought was that he loved her more than life itself.

Chapter Fourteen

Time sped up, the impact came, there were screams, the sound of ripping metal, then nothing. Miraculously, everything stopped. There was nothing. Then J.T. knew it was over and he was alive.

"Oh, damn it, damn it, damn it," Candice muttered beside him. And he knew she was alive.

The air bag was in his lap, torn out of the steering wheel, inflated and deflated so quickly he'd never even felt it happen. Then he looked at Candice, who was securely in her seat, staring at the air bag coming out of the dash and brown liquid everywhere. Coffee. All over the seat, soaking into her blouse and even in her hair.

She darted him a look, and he could see coffee on her nose. He would have laughed if he hadn't been so overwhelmingly thankful that they both seemed to have survived pretty much intact. Or so overwhelmingly aware of loving her. He loved her. God, he loved her.

"Are you okay?" he asked, his hand going out to catch at hers, damp from the coffee. He held on to her for dear life.

"I...I...think so," she said on a shudder. "That

truck, you were on the wrong side of the road, and it was…it was coming right at us.'' She swiped at her jacket with her free hand. ''And the coffee is all over.''

That was when he realized the nose of the car was at a steep downward angle, and the windshield was cracked. The car creaked slightly, then a voice was beside him, startling him.

''Hey, man, you okay in there?''

He turned and saw a young guy with a shaggy goatee and a shaved head peering in at them. It was then that he realized the driver's-side window was shattered, at the same time he felt Candice pull her hand out of his. ''Yeah, I think so.''

''You…you two had better get out, man. This thing can go down farther,'' he said, then he was tugging J.T.'s door open for him.

J.T. looked over at Candice, who was struggling to get her door open, but it wasn't giving. ''Here,'' he said, holding out his hand to her. ''Come on out this way.'' The car moved slightly and groaned again. ''Hurry up.''

Her hand was in his, and he edged himself out, then eased her out onto the soft ground beside him. They stood side by side in thick grass, still holding hands, and he was amazed that the car had stopped where it had. Another five feet, and it would have plunged another thirty feet down into ravine.

''You two are damn lucky,'' the kid said, echoing his own thoughts. ''And that truck, hey, I was right behind the rig, and he barely missed you. The guy just kept going, never even stopped.''

He felt Candice shudder, and he instinctively put his arm around her shoulders, pulling her to his side.

She didn't fight it at all. "Thanks for stopping," J.T. said.

"Ain't nothing, man."

He looked around. "Any idea where we can get a tow truck and a rental car?"

The kid frowned. "I can take you down the way with me to the garage, and I guess they can get what you need."

"That'd be great."

In a matter of minutes they were in an old beat-up pickup truck that was of indeterminate color, chugging back the way they'd come. Candice sat close to him, her hands in her lap, and he relished the feeling of her heat along his body, the way he could almost feel each breath she took.

He glanced at her, but she was staring straight ahead. "What's your name?" he asked the kid to fill in the spaces.

"Live Wire, er, well, my real name's Ray-Dean Olson, but my friends call me Live Wire. How about you?"

"J.T., and this is Candice."

"Glad you're both okay," he said.

"Me, too," J.T. breathed, and felt Candice tremble slightly.

"You two from Texas or something?"

"I'm from the Dallas area," J.T. told him.

"Thought so," Live Wire said, then pointed ahead of them. "There you go."

J.T. looked up and saw the sign Hank's Watering Hole.

Live Wire pulled into the graveled parking lot and across to the garage. "Believe me, it's better than it looks, and they'll have everything you need."

"I bet they will," J.T. said.

CANDICE STAYED in the pickup while J.T. and Live Wire talked to the mechanic at the huge garage. She watched J.T. and all she could think of was losing J.T., about a world without him in it, the way her world had been for eight years. Unbearable. Totally unbearable. She hugged herself tightly, and wished she could hold on to J.T. Just hold on and never let go. Then he was coming toward the truck, her whole world in one man. And that was staggering.

He pulled open the door and was looking up at her. "Darlin', they'll go and get your car, then have it towed to a dealer in Sacramento. Meanwhile, they're finding a rental car for us, which could take a while. I didn't figure you'd wanted to sit in the restaurant for a few hours, so I got you a room at the motel. You can clean up and catch your breath."

"What about...everything?"

"I'll take care of it," he said, then held out his hand. "Come on. Let's get you settled, then I can see what needs to be done."

She took his hand and climbed down out of the truck. J.T. turned and called out to the mechanic, "Let us know when the car gets here."

"Yes, sir," he called back.

"Live Wire?" The kid looked at him, and J.T. motioned him over to the two of them. He held out some money to him. "I can't tell you how much I appreciate your help."

"Hey, no, man," Live Wire said, both hands up, palms out. "I don't want nothing for what I did."

J.T. tucked the money in the pocket of the kid's shirt. "I want you to have it. Thanks."

"No problem. Just glad you and your wife aren't hurt."

Candice waited for J.T. to say something, but he just nodded. "We're going to be fine."

She stared at him. He'd told Live Wire she was his wife? Or had the boy just assumed it? She was startled by Live Wire talking right to her. "You got a good man there, ma'am, a real good man."

He turned from the two of them, heading back to his truck. Then J.T. put his arm around her as easily as if they'd been doing it for eight years. And they walked together across the graveled parking lot to the motel area.

"Cottage 10," he said, motioning to one of the units at the far end of the complex. "Over there."

He took a key out of his shirt pocket, and let her go to unlock and open the door. He let her duck in past him, then they were both inside and the door swung shut.

The room was small, with a double bed, a single dresser and a mirror over it. The floor was covered by striped carpet, and a door on the far side of the room opened to show a small bathroom. "It's not fancy, but it's clean," he said.

She looked at the room, then turned to J.T. "It's fine," she whispered.

"You clean up and I'll go and make some calls."

"There's a phone right there," she said, motioning to a phone on a side table by the bed.

"I'll call from the restaurant and give you some privacy," he said.

She didn't want him to leave, not now. She didn't want to be alone, to be without him. And without a word, she went toward him. With inches between them, she looked up at him. How could loving someone hurt so much? She lifted an unsteady hand and touched his chest, felt his heartbeat under her palm and shivered. "Don't leave me," she whispered.

He was very still, then ever so slowly, his hands lifted and framed her face. His thumbs brushed on her cheeks, and his eyes narrowed, as if he couldn't quite bear to look directly at her. "Are you sure?" he asked in a low, rough voice.

She never wanted anything more in her life. "Please."

His hands slipped to her throat, then her shoulders, and he was drawing her to him. And she went gladly. She fell into his arms, burying her face in the heat of his chest, and she simply inhaled him. She took in his scents, letting them seep into her soul. Then his hands started to move on her and she was lost in a place she'd only known once before, but had missed for an eternity.

The need was there, strong and urgent, and before she knew how it happened, her suit was on the floor around her ankles and J.T. was touching her, skin against skin. "Oh, darlin'," he breathed, and she trembled when he touched her breast through the fine material of her bra. She bit her lip, arching toward him, then suddenly she was in his arms.

He surrounded her, his heart beating against her cheek, a fire in her growing so rapidly that she was afraid it would consume her, but equally afraid that it would go away. That it would be denied to her since the last time they'd made love.

She clung to him, falling onto the bed with him, and suddenly he was on top of her, his weight and heat pressing on her. A welcome weight, a precious weight, until he shifted, and his body was alongside hers and she twisted toward him. She wanted no barriers, nothing to separate them, and she fumbled with his shirt.

"Damn it," she groaned in frustration when she couldn't get his shirt up.

He pushed back and, for a horrifying moment, the contact between them was gone completely. Panicking, she looked up, and her breath all but stopped when she saw J.T. stripping off his clothes. His shirt went first, exposing his naked chest, then he stepped out of his boots, kicking them away from the bed to land with soft thuds somewhere across the room.

His hazel eyes never left her face as he unsnapped his jeans and stripped off the denim. She ached at the sight before her, at how much she'd missed it, even though she'd only had it for such a short time. She remembered everything, every detail, and a need that had a life of its own drove her to sit up and reach out to J.T.

There was a flash of a smile before he came back to her, then he was by her, looking down at her, tracing the line of her collarbone with the tip of his finger. The simple touch made her tremble, and she gasped softly when his hand went lower, to her breasts. The wall between them was gone, she didn't know how and she didn't care.

All she wanted was his touch on her, his fingers teasing her nipples, drawing at a cord deep in her being that brought a life to her that was almost magical. The world didn't exist, just his touch. Nothing else mattered. Nothing.

Her hand covered his, pressing it to her breast,

then she rolled closer, pressing against him, relishing the feel of his desire against her stomach. He wanted her, and for that moment, that was enough. She was here, and his hands were drawing feelings from her that were new and exciting, and oddly scary at the same time. She tried to get closer, to disappear into him, to be a part of him, then he was kissing her while his hands roamed lower, and she lifted her hips to his touch.

She moaned softly, arching more, until the flat of his hand was pressed against her core. The feelings were too much, too brilliant and almost painfully intense. But they were just the beginning. She cried out as he invaded her with his fingers, finding her moist heat while he made slow circles against her with the heel of his hand.

"Oh, no," she groaned, lifting higher to have as much contact with him as was humanly possible. The feelings started to come in waves, higher and higher, and she strained against him. "Yes, yes." He moved faster and faster against her and when she was ready to explode, it all stopped.

She gasped, reaching for him, looking at him, ready to beg for what he was giving her, but she didn't have to. He was still there, shifting, moving over her, then she felt him against her, his strength testing her, then slowly, with exquisite gentleness, he entered her. Slowly, very slowly, until he filled her, and every part of her existence focused on him, just him.

He looked down at her, whispered, "I never forgot," then he was moving. He stroked her, in and out, the rhythm slow at first, then, as if he couldn't bear the pace, he started to move faster and faster.

The feelings were everywhere, filling every atom of her being, pulling her to him, filling the void in her life that she'd ignored for eight long years.

Then the universe narrowed to J.T., to his touch, to what he gave her, and two voices cried out at the same time. And two people were joined forever. Candice held on to him, afraid to let go in case she drifted away. But his arms were around her, his legs entwined with hers, and she was anchored firmly. She rode the waves of feeling with J.T., together, and as the shimmering shards of sensation started to diminish, she knew what love really was. This joining, this oneness, this sense that the whole world was theirs.

She snuggled into J.T., relishing the feel of his arms around her, his leg lying heavily over hers, and the steady beating of his heart against her cheek. She felt as if she'd finally found what she'd been looking for all her life. And as she let herself slip into a soft place of sleep, she was in awe of what love really was.

J.T. LOOKED AT CANDICE sleeping in his arms. She was the same, the girl he'd married eight years ago. But there was more now, more fire, more raw need. The hesitant virgin of eight years ago was a fiery, passionate woman. She sighed, shifting closer to him, her hand resting on his stomach while one leg shifted over his thigh. His wife.

He thought he'd had his fill, that he would be satisfied forever with what they'd had in the past hour, but that was a lie. As big a lie as the one he'd told himself before, that he could live without her,

that he didn't need her. A humongous lie that was
denied with every fiber in his being now.

He felt so connected to her at that moment that
he couldn't tell where he ended and she began. Becoming one. Wasn't that part of the wedding ceremony? He couldn't remember, but he knew it was
an absolute truth. She was part of him, buried deep
inside him, down in his soul. And if she wasn't
there, he wouldn't exist.

She moved again, and his whole body responded.
She was shifting, twisting around until he realized
they were face-to-face. Her hair tickled his nose,
then she moved back a bit. "I was wondering if you
were awake?" she said, her hand doing strange and
wonderful things to his skin, skimming over his
chest, then going lower to his stomach. He shuddered as she touched him, and he could have sworn
she laughed.

But he was too lost in the sensations, too con-
sumed by his need for her again, a need that he knew
now would never be satisfied, no matter how many
years they were together. He found her lips with his,
tasting her, drawing her essence into him, then she
found his strength and he gasped.

She did laugh that time, a seductively satisfied
sound that started to die as her hand moved on him.
He shifted onto his back, then his hands found her
waist and he lifted her over him and slowly eased
her down onto him.

She was over him, blotting out the rest of the
world with her being, and he moved his hands up
to her breasts. That made her groan, and when he
began to move, she shuddered softly and started to
match his rhythm with her own. And each motion

intensified the sensations until he was certain the pleasure would turn to pain.

He shifted, rolling over until he was over her this time, and each thrust drove the two of them higher and higher. "Yes, yes," Candice gasped, her hold on him tighter and tighter, then everything shattered. The explosion was beyond anything he'd ever known or ever imagined, and he went with her into a realm of such ecstasy that everything ceased to exist except the two of them.

Nothing in his life had prepared him for that moment, when he lost himself and found her. And knew that she was everything he was, he would be, or would ever want to be. She was his life.

A SOFT KNOCKING SOUND drew J.T. out of a sleep that was so luxurious, he grieved giving it up. Then he felt Candice pressed against his back, and he knew where he was. He knew what he had. The knocking sounded again, and she stirred, then settled.

Carefully, he eased out of bed, grabbed his jeans and stepped into them, then crossed to the door. He eased it back to the dusky light of early evening. The mechanic from the garage was there. "Sorry it took so long, sir, but the rental car's here, and the tow truck has the BMW. They're about to start back with it to the dealer, but they need some signatures before they can leave."

J.T. looked back into the room at Candice, curled like a kitten in the bed, still sound asleep. He lowered his voice, "Okay, tell them I'll be right there."

"Yes, sir," the man said, then walked off.

J.T. went inside, dressed quickly, and with one

lingering look at Candice, he left the small cottage and headed over to the garage. He wasn't at all certain what had just happened, but things had worked out after all. They were together, and he was going to make sure they stayed that way.

He started to whistle softly under his breath as he headed to the flatbed tow truck by the garage that had the twisted BMW on its bed. In less than twenty-four hours, things had all shifted, and he smiled as he realized that the annulment wouldn't happen after all. But not because they forgot or because there was a mix-up. It wouldn't happen, because they were married, and they were going to stay married. That felt right, very right, as right as the feeling of Candice in his arms.

Chapter Fifteen

Candice stirred and knew that she was alone even before she opened her eyes. She could feel a sense of aloneness that she knew now she'd felt for eight years, eight years of waking without J.T. by her side. She slowly opened her eyes as she rolled onto her side, and she knew she was right. Reaching out, she pressed her hand to the cool linen of the pillow that still held the impression of his head.

"J.T.?" she called, but there was no answer.

She pushed herself up, the cool air on her bare skin making her shake slightly. She grabbed the blanket, wrapped it around herself and got out of bed, crossing to the bathroom. But the room was empty.

She went back into the bedroom and sank onto the side of the bed. J.T. must have gone to make his calls. Probably one to Taylor telling him not to bother about the annulment. Married for eight years. That made her smile. It felt right. It felt perfect.

She spotted the phone and reached for it. She hesitated, not wanting to call her mother, but she knew who she wanted to talk to. She pressed in a number, then waited, and Whitney answered. She could have cried, she was so happy to hear her friend's voice over the line.

"Whitney? You're back?"

"Candice. Where are you? I called your house and your mother said you'd left a message about being gone for a while. What's going on?"

Candice didn't know where to start, but once she told Whitney about J.T. being at the wedding, the rest of the story spilled out. Whitney was silent during the telling, until Candice got to the point where she told her J.T. and she were still married.

"What? You and J.T.? You're still married?"

"Very. The annulment never went through."

"Candice, that's...that's..." She paused. "What is it? You tell me?"

Candice took a breath and said the truth. "It's a blessing in disguise."

"What?"

"Whitney, you know how it was, how crazy I was about J.T. Well, it never stopped. It sort of hibernated or something, but it's still there."

"You and J.T.?"

She talked quickly, telling her about their trip and about how it ended. When she finished, Whitney was silent for a long moment, then asked, "You still love him?"

"Absolutely. Strange, isn't it?"

"Not as strange as you loving J.T. and being engaged to Mark. What about him?"

"I feel so horrible about all of that. I mean, I never should have let it go as far as it did with him. I was so stupid, and it's horrible for both of us. I don't know how to tell him it was all a huge mistake." Her voice was shaking now. "It's going to hurt him, I know that. I just need to figure out how to let him down gently and hope that he'll understand.''

"Candice, what about your mother? You and Dylan have both told me how she feels about J.T. Has that changed?''

"No, nothing's changed. Nothing.''

"She's excited about you and Mark. How's she going to adjust to you and J.T.?''

Candice fell back on the bed and stared at the ceiling. "I don't know. I don't know anything anymore for sure, except I want this marriage and I want it so badly it's scary.''

"You love him that much?''

"More than I can say,'' she said.

"Then I'm behind you, for what it's worth.''

"It's worth a lot.'' She closed her eyes. "You know something, I think your Uncle Karl likes J.T. They really got along well at the wedding.''

"Uncle Karl's smart about people.''

"Smarter than I've been,'' she said with a sigh.

There was a sound outside, then the door opened and J.T. was there. J.T. dressed in his jeans and boots and shirt, with the Stetson pulled low. But not low enough to hide his expression. He looked distant, almost cold, and it shocked her.

"I have to go,'' she said into the phone. "I'll see you when I get back.''

"You'd better see me and fill me in on everything.''

"Sure,'' she said, never looking away from J.T. as she hung up the phone and stood. "Where were you?'' she asked.

J.T. stayed by the door and suddenly she felt awkward and uneasy. "Arranging for the car to be towed and signing for the rental car." He tossed a set of keys onto the bed. "It's all yours."

She didn't understand. "What?"

"The rental car. It's yours. Go on back home and I'll make sure the annulment is done in a week. You've got my word on it."

She could barely take in what he was saying. "The annulment?"

"You bet. Then it's over. This..." He cut the air with one hand. "Forget it. It was a mistake."

She knew there should be tremendous pain, but she was numb. Nothing was happening. She was watching J.T. tell her that everything was a mistake, that they'd get the annulment, and she wasn't feeling anything. That was wrong, very wrong, but she didn't know what to do.

"You...you're..."

"I'm making this easy for both of us. It's a mistake and it's done. I'm leaving. You take the car. I called Taylor, and he says he can do the annulment in a week. You'll get the papers."

She stared at him, the man who had made love to her, and heard him saying it was nothing. The pain should be monumental, but it wasn't even there. There was a humming sound somewhere, a strange monotone in her ears, and even though J.T. was still talking, she couldn't understand a thing he was saying.

She sank onto the bed, waited until he quit talking, and looked up at him. "Are you through?"

He stared at her...hard. Then he nodded. "Yes, I'm through."

"Then leave," she said.

His mouth thinned and he hesitated, his hand on the doorknob. "A Montgomery to the end," he said.

"Leave," she repeated.

"The rental car's outside. I'm riding with the tow truck driver. They'll have your car at the BMW dealer in Sacramento."

She stared at him. "No, don't leave," she said. "Stay right there."

She stood, letting the sheet drop as she reached for her clothes. She dressed in front of him, not caring what he saw or what she felt. She dressed, turned and grabbed her purse without bothering to comb her hair or put on makeup.

"I'm leaving." She grabbed the keys off the bed. "I'm the one walking out. You stay here and do whatever the hell you want to do. I just don't care," she said and walked to the door. She stopped a few feet from J.T. then said the one thing she knew would hurt. "My mother and father were actually right. This was a huge mistake."

She saw his expression tighten, but the brief flash of satisfaction at making him hurt a bit was gone when he nodded. "Damn straight."

She ducked past him and grabbed the door, jerking it open. Without looking back, she left, closed the door without slamming it and walked out onto the gravel. A blue Chevy was parked a few feet away and she crossed to it.

She got in, put the key in the ignition and thankfully the car started. She backed up, turned around and drove to the frontage road, then out onto the highway to go west, to go back home.

She stared straight ahead, wondering how a dream could have turned into a nightmare in such a short time. J.T. had come back to Montgomery Beach twenty-four hours ago and brought the nightmare with him. He'd let her think it could be a dream, then he turned it right back into a nightmare. And he left her with nothing.

She started to shake and had to pull over onto a side road. She'd just parked when everything fell apart. She hugged her arms around herself, but the pain rushed at her, overtaking her, and the tears came in great gulping sobs. It felt as if she'd die, then she knew she wasn't going to die. She'd live and learn how to exist with a part of her soul gone forever.

J.T. WALKED AWAY from the cottage ten minutes later with Candice's words echoing deep inside him.

"I feel so horrible about all of that. I mean, I never should have let it go as far as it did with him. I was so stupid, and it's horrible for both of us."

He'd just gotten to the door of the cottage right then, and heard her talking. He'd been stopped dead by what he heard.

"I don't know how to tell him it was all a huge mistake. It's going to hurt him, I know that."

Hurt him? It was killing him. He kept walking toward the tow truck. She was miserable about what had happened, just the way she'd been eight years ago, but this time she had Mark.

"I just need to figure out how to let him down gently and hope that he'll understand."

He'd forced this. If he hadn't, they wouldn't be here, and they wouldn't have made love. He'd done it again. He'd wanted her and taken her. And she regretted it.

"No, nothing's changed. Nothing." Nothing had changed, certainly not just because he loved her. Nothing. He nodded to the tow-truck driver, then climbed into the cab and closed the door.

"I want this marriage and I want it so badly it's scary."

She wanted her marriage to Mark. Damn it all, he should have been noble. He should have sent her back to Mark with his blessings. As long as she was happy, he'd be happy. That almost made him laugh. What a joke. He hated the thought of her being with Mark. And he hated the thought of never having her again. Noble? Not even close.

And it was a joke that he'd promised Karl Delaney to not hurt her on purpose. The man had said nothing about her hurting him. And, God, it hurt. Giving up hurt like hell.

But he'd made a deal. If he couldn't make it work, he'd let it go. And he was letting it go.

CANDICE ARRIVED BACK in Montgomery Beach late that night and went straight up to her room as quietly as possible. The last thing she wanted was to face her mother at that moment in her life. She took two sleeping pills, then stayed in a hot shower until she felt drowsy. She got out and crawled into bed, letting sleep claim her, and fell into a place where she didn't have to think.

When morning came, Candice woke with a horrible headache and a sense of dread that was oppressive. Everything had changed, and nothing she could do would make things better. Nothing. But she had some things she had to do, parts of her life that she had to end as quickly and as gently as possible.

She dressed in jeans and a loose sweater, then quietly went downstairs in her bare feet. No one stirred, but she could smell coffee in the kitchen and headed for it. A cup of coffee, then she'd call Mark. She went to the back of the house and stepped into the kitchen, the stone floor of the cavernous room cold under her feet.

She looked up and stopped dead in her tracks from shock. She hadn't heard anyone stirring, but she was facing her mother sitting at the glass-topped table in the breakfast area. And right beside her was Karl Delaney.

She must have gasped, because the two of them turned, the look of shock on their faces as clear as her own shock. Her mother and Karl. Then she realized they weren't just sitting at the breakfast table, they were holding hands, and they were both in their robes.

God, the world had gone crazy. Her mother and Karl?

Karl stood quickly while she felt as if she'd fallen down the rabbit hole and come face-to-face with the Queen of Hearts and the Mad Hatter. But this wasn't a fairy tale.

"Mother?" she whispered.

Grace stood quickly and crossed to Candice. "Oh, dear, I didn't hear you come in. How…how long have you…?" She was panic stricken, Grace Montgomery out of control. Another first. "I…I can explain."

Karl touched Grace's shoulder. "No, it is I who should explain. I am the stranger in this house."

Grace turned to him, tiny and delicate in front of

the tall man. "Karl, no, that's not true. You belong here."

He smiled down at her, an indulgent smile. "Oh, Grace, you make me so happy."

"I'm leaving," Candice said. This couldn't be happening.

"No," both of them said at the same time.

"Mother, you and Karl...you two..."

Grace crossed to where Candice stood by the door and took her hand. "Darling, this is my fault. Karl wanted to tell you, but I..." She shook her head. "He's been so impatient, but I just couldn't."

"Mother, are you saying you and Karl are having an affair?"

Grace colored at the question. "Candice, I know what you must think, but—"

"Mother, I don't know what to think," she said honestly, trying to deal with the strangest feeling of free falling and having no idea how to stop.

Grace reached behind her and found Karl's hand. "Darling, I can explain, and I want you to understand. You have to understand." She shook her head. "This is so difficult, and I don't want to hurt anyone, especially you."

Karl had been silent for a few moments, but spoke up then. "Grace, it is I who should do this," he repeated. "I must explain to Candice."

Candice looked from Karl to her mother and knew there were no explanations needed. She'd caught Karl and her mother on "the morning after" and her mother looked like a woman in love. Tears were there, but not because of hurt, but because the two of them had obviously found what she knew she'd never have.

Everything made sense to her now or, at least, her mother's actions at the wedding and yesterday morning all made sense. Karl being there every time she turned around recently. Karl talking to her mother, being close, but never touching...until now. She shook her head, turning from them to cross to the counter and get coffee. She needed coffee to help her try to find some sense in her life.

She poured a cup, but when she finally turned, only Karl was there, standing straight in a dove-gray robe, his blue eyes filled with concern. She leaned back against the counter and sipped the strong black liquid, letting it filter into her, but it didn't reach a coldness in her middle.

"Karl, let me make this easy for both of us." She spoke a truth that she'd known all her life, yet never quite faced. "I know my mother and father didn't love each other, not really. Oh, maybe at first, but after that, they were just together. And if you're making my mother happy, it's okay." Another truth came out of its own volition. "She has never been happy...until now."

He came closer, a slight smile on his lips, but that concern was still there. "How do you know what your mother and father felt for each other?"

She bit her lip. How could she say that she'd finally felt love and knew that what her mother and father had had was nothing close to the real thing. "I know." She sipped more coffee, needing heat inside her, but not feeling it.

"No judgments, no thoughts that this will not be...how would you put it, proper? That a mere tailor is not fit for a Montgomery? A common man?"

She was almost able to hear her father saying that

very sentence with his disdain, but instead of using the word *tailor,* he'd used *cowboy.* "You're far from common," she said, and another simple truth was there, despite what her father had always said. "And if you really love her, nothing else matters."

"Oh, I love her." Then he came closer to her. "You are so wise," he murmured. "I am proud of you."

Why did it mean so much to her that this man was proud of her, even if it was for something most people knew all their lives? "Thank you."

He tapped her chin lightly with one finger. "This is quite remarkable."

Her mother in love, really in love? Yes, that was remarkable. "So, you and Mother, you two, you…"

"Yes, we two." That smile was there again. "Now, there is one more thing we wish to tell you, but Grace needs to be here for this." He turned and called, "Grace. It is time."

She looked at him, then her mother was there at his side, slipping her hand into his with a heart-wrenching familiarity. Boy, nothing was the same anymore. This woman facing her looked like a teen-ager, so happy and relieved, then she looked at Karl as he glanced at her. And she ached for what they had. What she'd never have now.

"Well, what else is there?" she asked.

Karl and Grace looked at each other, then Grace said softly, "Candice, darling, you'd better sit down for this."

GRACE AND KARL LEFT an hour later, and Candice wondered if the world had gone mad. She'd phoned Whitney and Dylan, leaving a message for the two of them to call her as soon as they could. Then she left the house, walked out across the back terrace, over the lawn in her bare feet, and went down to the beach.

The sun was warm on her skin, but that chill was still there. She walked to the water's edge, staring out at the horizon as the sun crept higher in the sky. Another day, unlike any other day she'd ever known. She hugged her arms around herself, knowing she had to go back to the house and call Mark. But she couldn't make herself move. She had so much to absorb, so much to adjust to. She wondered if she'd ever be able to find her balance again.

She knew she wasn't alone at the same moment she heard someone speak to her. But it wasn't her name. She was hallucinating this time. She knew she had to be at the sound of a low, roughly whispered, "Darlin'."

She closed her eyes, the imaginings in her mind driving her slightly crazy. She couldn't have heard what she thought she heard. And she believed that, until it came again, this time closer to her.

"Darlin'?"

She slowly turned and J.T. was there. The morning sun showed the man she loved, totally and completely, with all of her heart. He was just a few feet from her, a white silk shirt open at the throat, molded to his broad shoulders, those jeans and his boots pressing into the sand. The Stetson shadowed his eyes from the sun, but did nothing to lessen the impact of his gaze on her.

This couldn't be happening. She backed up, ready to run away from the madness, but he stopped her. "The maid said she saw you coming down here."

A pain so wrenching that she could barely breathe gripped her middle. He couldn't be here. He couldn't expect her to talk calmly, as if nothing had happened. Then she knew why he'd come back. And the pain grew. "You...you have papers for me?"

He shook his head. "Not yet."

"What are you doing here?"

He took a step toward her, and she had to force herself not to run. "I came after you."

"What?" she whispered.

"You said the last time that I never came after you." He moved even closer. "This time I came after you."

"Why?" She barely got out the single word around the tightness in her throat.

He exhaled roughly, then came closer still. "Don't run," he said softly. "Listen to me."

She couldn't have run to save her life, which was just about what she was thinking of trying to do right then. Save her life. With him this close, she was within a heartbeat of losing whatever control she'd managed to find. "I thought you were in London, or with Vonya, or getting the annulment papers drawn up."

"I was on my way to London, and I almost got on the Concorde in New York, but I couldn't. I realized that eight years ago, I left. I didn't go after you. And it's been eight long years of emptiness." His eyes narrowed, as if minimizing a pain of some sort. "I couldn't do that again. I couldn't make that mistake." He laughed, a rough, humorless sound that echoed slightly off the bluffs. "God, I couldn't live another day without you, much less another eight years."

She was starting to shake, and she had to hug her arms around her middle to try to keep from falling apart. "I don't..." She touched her tongue to her cold lips. "I don't understand."

He was closer, so close she felt the heat of his breath brush her face when he exhaled before saying, "Understand this, Candice Montgomery. I know that you're planning on marrying Mark, that you regret what we've had, but I'm here to tell you I'm not giving up. And I won't until I know there's no hope for us."

She couldn't believe what he was saying, or what she thought he was trying to say. "No hope?"

He shook his head. "They say hope dies hard, well, mine's going to die a long, slow, agonizing death."

"Why?"

He looked right at her, then he touched her, his hands resting on her shoulders, but the space still separated them. "Because, darlin', I love you."

She knew now that she was truly mad. "You...you love me?"

"I know it might be too late, but I couldn't let it go. I got on a plane back here and I'm here to tell you that I love you. I'll take you any way I can have you, no conditions, no ultimatums. Any way at all." That smile was there, but it looked uneasy. A man who built an empire, a man who never lost, looked unsure of himself. "Just tell me I'm in the running, at least?"

Candice reached out and touched J.T. on the jaw, felt the prickle of new beard there and ran her finger down to the hollow at his throat. His pulse was racing. Yes, he was afraid. And she knew the truth right then.

She moved closer to him, lifting her face, and a smile came from deep in her soul. "Cowboy, you're not only in the running, you're the only runner."

The next thing she knew, she was in his arms, and his lips found hers. A kiss unlike any other kiss they'd ever shared. He loved her! She held on to him, barely believing it, yet her whole soul knew it was true.

She kept her arms around his neck, but moved back a bit so she could look into his eyes. "J. T. Watson, I love you."

He startled her when he threw back his head and yelled, "Yes!" to the skies, and he was spinning her around and around in his arms.

Then he stopped to give her a quick, fierce kiss before he drew back. "My wife," he said softly.

"Forever," she whispered.

"Forever," he repeated. "And that starts now." He looked around the beach, then back down at her. "I want you, and I want you now."

"The house is ours," she said, aching to be with him again.

"What about your mother?"

"She's not there," she said, unable to believe that she'd forgotten about her mother and Karl. "You won't believe this," she said, never letting go of him as they headed for the steps to go up to the house. "But my mother and Karl, well…" She stopped and turned to face him from the bottom stair, bringing her to his eye level. "Mother and Karl, they're together."

"Together where?"

"No, I mean really together. J.T., they're in love."

He looked shocked for a moment, then grinned, an expression that melted her heart. "Well, I'll be damned. That was what he was talking about."

"Who, talking about what?"

"Karl. We commiserated about woman trouble. Your mother was obviously his 'trouble.'" His smile slipped just a bit. "Maybe she'll understand about us now. Your father never would have, but...."

She got closer, circling his neck with her arms, bringing her face to within inches of his. "J.T., there's one more thing you should know about me. My father likes you...a lot."

He frowned at her. "Darlin', you're crazy."

"No, confused and shocked, and very, very much in love with my husband, but I'm not crazy." She kissed him lightly, skimming her lips over his, then drawing back. "I just found out something, something about Karl and my mother. They just told me before they left."

J.T. was starting to look bothered, and she wanted to smooth the traces of frown off his face. "Darlin', just tell me so we can get up to the house, and I can show you how much I love you."

She shivered slightly with anticipation, but she had to tell him this one last thing. She didn't know how to say it, so she simply told him, "Karl's my father." His obvious shock was nothing compared to what her shock had been an hour ago, but now it seemed right someway. It was easy to say, "My mother and he, they were in love a long time ago when my father, John, and she were having terrible problems. Karl was there, and they fell in love and she got pregnant.

"She did what she had to do. She stayed with John, and for all practical purposes, I was his daughter. Karl wanted her to go with him, but she couldn't. She was terrified that John would take Dylan and she'd never see her son again. So she stayed, and she became the perfect wife. And so sad." She swallowed hard. "John Montgomery was really good to me, despite everything. He loved me. But all the time, Karl was there, watching out for me...and for my mother."

"You have no idea how he watched out for you," J.T. whispered.

She didn't understand, but she knew they had a lifetime to figure things out. "He's been here all my life. He wanted Whitney raised here after her parents died, and that meant he could be there for me."

"Oh, darlin', he's quite a man to stay like that and watch from a distance."

She could feel tears now, but she didn't fight them. "He couldn't bear to be very far from my mother, either, even if he couldn't have her. She's always been his one and only love. And now they're going to be together. After all these years."

J.T. brushed at her tears. "After all these years," he echoed. "I know how they feel." He framed her face with his hands. "I knew I liked that man. How could I not like him, when he's the father of my one and only love? My wife."

Epilogue

Labor Day Weekend

The wedding was small, with just family and close friends, but the bride and groom were so happy, the others could feel it in the air.

J.T. was out of his jeans and boots and in a custom-made tux again. Candice was radiant in a simple ivory silk dress that brought out her golden tan from the days they'd spent riding on the ranch. The highlights in her silky hair shone. J.T. could barely take his eyes off his wife. His heart lurched when she smiled at Dylan and Whitney, when she hugged Patrick and teased Jack and Sandi about getting a baby brother or sister for the boy. The way she patted Whitney's expanding middle, patiently waiting to feel the baby kick against her hand.

Even when she was laughing with Steffi and helping her put out the appetizers on the glass tables scattered around the terrace at the back of the Montgomery mansion, J.T. stood back, just watching, in awe of the fact that she was his wife. The one and only love in his life.

Then she looked at him with those incredibly blue

eyes, eyes that were so much like her father's, then she was coming toward him carrying two glasses of champagne. She offered him one and smiled at him.

"Isn't it all perfect?" she said, filled with obvious joy and excitement. "Everything just worked out."

He leaned toward her. "It would be perfect if we were back at the ranch, alone. Now, that's perfect."

"Soon, cowboy, soon," she whispered.

"Not soon enough, darlin'."

"Friends, family," Dylan said as he stood with a glass of champagne in his hand. "Can I have your attention."

J.T. looked at his friend, standing by the table with the elegant wedding cake centered on it. Dylan, a married man, soon to be a father. J.T. smiled at him. And Jack, Sandi and Patrick, a real family. What a way life had of figuring things out for people who didn't have a clue what they really wanted.

He moved closer to Candice and took her hand, loving the feeling of her fingers laced with his. The cool metal of the simple wedding band on her finger, one as close to the original as they could find. He needed that connection with her, and loved the way she leaned against him, her shoulder on his shoulder, as she watched her brother.

"Now's the time for the best man to offer a toast," Dylan said, lifting his goblet. "And since I'm the best man, it's my pleasure to be here with everyone who I love, who's important to me." His gaze went from Whitney, to Jack and Sandi and Patrick, then over to J.T. and Candice.

Then to the bride and groom. Karl, in an elegant tuxedo of his own making, and Grace, in a gown done in lace the color of a pale pink rose. He lifted his glass higher. "To my mother, for all she's been to me, and to Karl, for making her so happy." He inclined his head to his stepfather. "Thank you for everything you've done for this family."

Karl held on to Grace and smiled at Dylan, then nodded. "Thank you for letting me become part of this family."

Then Dylan looked at J.T. and Candice. "Also, to my sister and her husband, one of the best men in the world. Thank you for making my sister so happy."

"It's the easiest thing I've ever done," he said.

"My turn," Candice said and lifted her glass toward Grace and Karl. "To my mother. I love you, and..." J.T. saw the slight unsteadiness in her hand and heard the catch in her voice as she finished, "To my new father. I'm so glad you're in our lives."

Karl Delaney smiled at Candice, raised his glass, and the rest of the guests clapped.

Then Candice turned to face J.T. "And to my husband, the only cowboy I know who looks this good in a tuxedo." The guests laughed and clapped, and only J.T. heard the rest of her toast. "My one and only love."

At Karl Delaney's tux shop you get more than a bow
tie and cummerbund, you get free advice on your love
life. As Karl says, "You don't own a tux shop for forty
years and not know a little something about romance."

*Join friends Dylan, Jack and J.T. as they pick up their
tuxes and find surprise messages in their pockets.*

SUDDENLY A DADDY
Mindy Neff April 1999

THE LAST TWO BACHELORS
Linda Randall Wisdom May 1999

COWBOY IN A TUX
Mary Anne Wilson June 1999

**DELANEY'S GROOMS—Tuxedo rentals and sales—
matchmaking included!**

Available at your favorite retail outlet.

HARLEQUIN®
SUPERROMANCE

Due to popular reader demand, Harlequin Superromance® is expanding from 4 to 6 titles per month!

Starting May 1999, you can have more of the kind of stories that you love!

- **Longer, more complex plots**
- **Popular themes**
- **Lots of characters**
- **A great romance!**

Available May 1999 at your favorite retail outlet.

HARLEQUIN®
Makes any time special ™

Look us up on-line at: http://www.romance.net

HSR4TO6

 HARLEQUIN®

AMERICAN ◆ ROMANCE®

COMING NEXT MONTH

#781 DADDY UNKNOWN by Judy Christenberry
4 Tots for 4 Texans
Tuck was thrilled to see Alexandra Logan back in Cactus, Texas—until
she told him she had a little problem. She was four months pregnant—
and, thanks to a slight amnesia problem, she didn't know who was the
man responsible!

#782 LIZZIE'S LAST-CHANCE FIANCÉ by Julie Kistler
The Wedding Party
Bridesmaid Lizzie Muldoon had resolved to attend the society wedding
stag, but somehow ended up with a *fake* fiancé! Groomsman Joe Bellamy
was the lucky guy for Lizzie. And she couldn't convince anyone he was
not her future husband—including herself....

#783 INSTANT DADDY by Emily Dalton
A whirlwind romance with a stranger resulted in the best part of
Cassie Montgomery's life—her son, Tyler. She never expected to see her
mystery man's picture in a magazine—advertising for a wife! Breathless,
Cassie replied. Would Adam Baranoff remember her—and welcome her
gift of instant fatherhood?

#784 AND BABIES MAKE TEN by Lisa Bingham
New Arrivals
A trip to the sperm bank and suddenly Casey Fairchild found herself
leaving the fast track behind and taking a job in a tiny Midwest town.
But life was anything but dull when her boss turned out to be a sexy
stud—and the father of quintuplets!

Look us up on-line at: http://www.romance.net